LIFE SENTENCE

Andrew Neiderman

severn House

This first world edition published in Great Britain 2007 by
SEVERN HOUSE PUBLISHERS LTD of
9–15 High Street, Sutton, Surrey SM1 1DF.
This first world edition published in the USA 2008 by
SEVERN HOUSE PUBLISHERS INC of
595 Madison Avenue, New York, N.Y. 10022.
This first trade paperback edition published 2008 by
SEVERN HOUSE PUBLISHERS, London and New York.

British Library Cataloguing in Publication Data

Neiderman, Andrew
  Life sentence
  1. Older people - Crimes against - Fiction 2. Serial murder
  investigation - Fiction 3. Scientists - Fiction
  4. Detectives - Fiction 5. Suspense fiction
  I. Title
  813.5'4[F]

  ISBN-13: 978-0-7278-6557-1   (cased)
  ISBN-13: 978-1-84751-029-7   (trade paper)

All Severn House titles are printed on acid-free paper.

Typeset by Palimpsest Book Production Ltd.,
Grangemouth, Stirlingshire, Scotland.
Printed and bound in Great Britain by
MPG Books Ltd., Bodmin, Cornwall.

For my brother-in-law Richard who will always remain a
star in our sky

Prologue

The Intensive Care floor of what the employees called the Oakland Clinic, for lack of any other nomenclature, was dimly lit. It had the look and feel of the wee hours even though it was just a little past eight in the evening: longer shadows thinning into spider webs over the milk-white plaster walls, no one walking the halls or visiting patients.

Currently, there were four patients who had been admitted on the floor, two nurses and a nurse's aide. The two nurses were watching a rerun of *I Love Lucy* on a television set just to the right of the heart monitors, one of which had just flat-lined. Neither nurse noticed.

They both laughed aloud, their voices reverberating and seemingly absorbed in the nearby walls that also digested the blinking glow of the television screen.

At the far end of the hall, Mrs Littleton, the nurse's aide, stepped out of a patient's room and walked casually down to the nurses' station. She watched the last few moments of the segment of *I Love Lucy* and when the commercial came on she, like a school teacher getting her students' attention, tapped the counter with her digital thermometer.

Freda Rosen looked up first, visibly annoyed at being addressed in such a manner.

'What?'

Keeping her stern, school teacher's expression, Mrs Littleton nodded at the monitor to the right, the one with the flat line.

'When did that happen, I wonder?' Shirley Cole asked.

Mrs Littleton shrugged. 'I'm not a nurse, but I anticipated it. I thought he was looking a darker shade of blue for the last few hours.'

'Darker?' Shirley looked at Freda Rosen who rose and unfolded her body as if she were eighty, pressing down on her lower back and groaning. 'I swear that chiropractor is worthless,' she declared, rubbing her lower back vigorously. It looked like she was pumping blood into it.

'You get what you pay for,' Mrs Littleton said, the corners of her thick wormy lips disappearing into her bloated cheeks and round chin. Her mouth looked like one formed in a ball of clay by a child inserting four tightly pressed together fingers. At least that was what Shirley envisioned.

'I don't pay for it,' Freda eagerly bragged. 'He's my daughter's brother-in-law.'

'Exactly,' Mrs Littleton said with a shrug. 'You pay nothing. You get nothing.'

Shirley Cole laughed. Her laugh was a singular guttural sound that rose like a bronchial cough and died just outside her mouth. She rose, too and the three of them started down the corridor.

'You forgot the pads,' Mrs Littleton said and nodded back toward the desk.

'We didn't forget them,' Shirley said. 'What's the point of resuscitating this one?'

The three entered the room of patient Ronald Sutter. Freda confirmed he had passed away and Shirley turned off the heart monitor.

They stared at the elderly man who looked like he was shrinking right before their eyes, melting in the bed and threatening to become one putrid glob of ooze.

'I swear he was at least ten to fifteen pounds heavier two days ago,' Mrs Littleton said. 'I'd like to know more about all this.'

'What for?' Freda asked, still smarting from Mrs Littleton's clever comment about her son-in-law's value. 'Curiosity killed the cat.'

'Yes, but she's right. He was at least that much heavier,' Shirley Cole said.

'Actually, from the sight of him that first day and the condition he was in, it took him a lot longer to expire than I had expected,' Freda admitted.

'You're both sure this isn't something we can catch, something infectious?' Mrs Littleton asked.

'Of course we're sure,' Shirley said. 'How ridiculous.'

'How can you be so sure?' Mrs Littleton pursued. 'By your own admittance, you know very little, and why is it that they're all so elderly? I mean, they're not just in their sixties or in their seventies. They're all like eighty or even ninety! Where do they come from? How come there are no members of anyone's family visiting or inquiring?'

The two nurses glared at her, both with similar disapproval in their eyes.

'You're asking too many questions. You signed under the same conditions we did and you've accepted the money,' Freda reminded her.

'I know. I just . . .' She looked at the dead man. 'I never saw anything like it. I overheard Mr Sutter ask Dr Hoffman how this had happened to him? What did he mean? How what had happened? Old age? He asked that only the day before yesterday. Mr Sutter was here only four days, I think,' Mrs Littleton said.

'Three and a half, but who's counting?' Shirley said.

Freda raised her eyebrows. 'Do I have to tell you who's counting, who wants to know about each and every heart-beat?'

'No,' Shirley said and brought the sheet up and over Ronald Sutter and then turned sharply to Mrs Littleton as something she said registered. 'What do you mean, you overheard? You were eavesdropping, snooping on a conversation between the doctor and his patient?'

'Absolutely not. I was just getting some fresh linen and . . .'

'If you two don't mind, let's stop chattering over a corpse,' Freda said.

The three started out.

'Don't either of you have nightmares about any of this?' Mrs Littleton asked. When Freda said, 'chattering over a corpse' it made her envision the dead man listening with his eyes turning a rancid yellow.

'It's better not to think or talk about it,' Shirley muttered. 'If you really can't do that, you should ask to be relieved of the duty. And Freda's right, you know you shouldn't be talking about any of it and you shouldn't be repeating things you've overheard, accidentally or not.'

'I didn't say I couldn't stop thinking or talking about it, and I wouldn't talk about any of this with anyone else but you two.'

'If you did, that wouldn't be wise,' Freda said, narrowing her eyes when she looked at her. 'Not wise at all.'

'I don't like threats. I won't stand for that,' Mrs Littleton snapped back.

Freda stopped walking and so did the other two. 'Are you going to stand there and tell us that you had no sense of a threat when the conditions were explained to you?' Freda asked Mrs Littleton.

Mrs Littleton looked at Shirley. 'Well, not exactly a threat, no.'

Shirley shook her head. 'This isn't good,' she said. 'If they hear about any complaining . . .'

'I'm not complaining,' Mrs Littleton said emphatically.

'Sounds like a complaint to me,' Freda muttered.

Mrs Littleton looked at her, the fear forming visibly in her trembling lips. 'It's not a complaint. I'm just . . .'

'Talking too much,' Freda said. She started walking again and the other two joined her.

'I'll admit this much,' Freda continued. 'I'm not so sure we were smart choosing this shift. In my experience terminal patients die more during the late evening hours for some stupid reason and then we have all that paperwork. The other two have an easier ride.'

'Are you making the call or am I this time?' Shirley asked instead of continuing the topic.

'I think it's my turn,' Freda said.

She went to the phone.

Shirley took her seat again and turned back to the television set.

The commercial had ended and the show resumed.

'I swear,' Shirley told Mrs Littleton. 'I've seen this one ten times if I've seen it once, and I don't laugh any less.'

'Ain't that the truth? Some things just last and last,' Freda said.

'Unlike our patients.'

They both laughed. Mrs Littleton looked away so they couldn't see the disapproval in her face.

Freda picked up the receiver, poked the numbers with the pen in her hand, waited a moment and then announced Sutter's death. She listened and then she hung up. She looked a little ashen.

'What?' Shirley Cole asked her.

'He was very angry. I mean . . . very. He said this can't continue, making it sound like it's our fault somehow.'

'What can't continue?' Mrs Littleton asked. 'Very old men dying? How could that possibly be our fault?'

Neither nurse answered her.

'It might mean no more patients, no more clinic, no more high paying jobs,' Freda said.

'Damn. I was looking forward to having the down payment soon on that townhouse in Monroe. Bobby would have such a shorter commute to his office in Manhattan,' Shirley added.

'Maybe things will turn out better for the other three,' Freda said.

'Better? Looking at them and what's being done for them, what could be better for them than their dying in their sleep?' Mrs Littleton asked.

'No matter what happens, we should ask for some sort of bonus, don't you think?' Shirley asked Freda.

'We oughta get a lot more than we get,' Freda agreed.

'Yeah,' Mrs Littleton said, still steaming from the way the two of them had clamped down on her and ignored her, 'you two work so hard it's criminal.'

'It's not how hard we work; it's what we do,' Freda said sternly.

'I wouldn't talk like that, if I were you,' Shirley said softly. 'Neither of you,' she added, looking pointedly at Mrs Littleton.

Freda looked at her, glanced at Mrs Littleton and then looked away.

Shirley laughed at Lucy's antics on television. Freda and Mrs Littleton both turned back to the television set and then all three laughed harder than they had before. It was as if they needed to soak themselves in humor after just the subtle hint of something threatening.

Freda insisted Lucy never got old.

'Unlike our patients,' Shirley muttered and they all laughed again. It was clear that for the moment at least no one could say anything that wouldn't be funny.

The sound of their laughter resonated in the hallway and echoed down the long corridors of darkness through which the remaining patients were slipping quickly into their own eternal night.

All but one that was.

'I'll start on Mr Sutter's report,' Shirley said. 'And we'll get him down to the morgue.'

Freda decided to take a walk. Unlike her last nursing job, this one required so little physically, she actually gained weight.

'Good. I'm getting some exercise,' she announced and started down the corridor. She glanced in two of the rooms, vaguely interested in the remaining patients, and continued on as if she were window shopping for a patient on whom to practice a procedure.

When she reached the end of the corridor, she turned and started back, glancing into room four. The empty bed stopped her in her tracks.

'Huh?' she said as if someone had spoken.

Cautiously, skeptically, she entered the room and gazed about. It was empty.

'How?'

She turned and hurried back up the corridor, her heels snapping like tiny firecrackers on the cream-colored tile, the muscles in her calves bobbing like a yo-yo.

'Something's wrong,' she announced. 'Mr Morris is not in his room.'

'Not in his bed?' Mrs Littleton said.

'No, not in his room. He detached the monitor. Why didn't we see that?'

They all looked at it.

'I was concentrating on the report,' Shirley explained. She gave Mrs Littleton a look of chastisement.

'Well, it couldn't have been too long ago. Maybe while we were attending Mr Sutter,' Mrs Littleton offered. 'At least I saw he had flat-lined.'

'Neither of you is listening to me. Didn't you two hear what I said? I said Mr Morris is not in his bed and not in his room,' Freda repeated with more urgency and concern.

'Did you check the bathroom?' Shirley asked her.

'Of course. Besides, how could he get up and go to the bathroom?'

Mrs Littleton smiled as if Freda had been saying the most ridiculous things and turned to Shirley who smiled.

'I'm not kidding, you two. Go look for yourselves.'

They stopped smiling.

'The man was nearly comatose,' Shirley said. 'The last pulse I took was somewhere in the forties. His blood pressure was barely recordable. I actually anticipated him going before Sutter.'

'I know what he was and what he wasn't,' Freda said. 'I know every patient on this floor down to his or her last few drops of blood, don't I?'

'OK, OK,' Shirley said and nodded at Mrs Littleton. They both rose and the three of them hurried down the corridor and paused at the doorway of room four. They gazed around.

'How the hell?' Mrs Littleton said.

Shirley shook her head.

'He couldn't have walked past us, could he?'

They turned to the doorway at the end of the corridor and then hurried through it.

Down the stairway on the first set of steps, they saw the hospital gown.

'What did he do, run out of here naked?' Shirley asked.

Freda thought about the janitor's closet off the stairway before the other two did and went to it.

'Buzzy leaves a set of overalls in here and boots for when he washes down the driveway and the ambulance. Look. They're gone.'

'How could he just get up and walk away in his condition?' Shirley wondered. 'Now, I'm beginning to have those nightmares you mentioned,' she told Mrs Littleton.

'Do you think someone came in and snatched him?' Mrs Littleton asked.

The two nurses thought and both shook their heads.

'They would have made too much noise and how would they get in the building?' Freda asked.

'If any of them were terminal, he was,' Shirley repeated.

'Exactly. But how could he rebound and that quickly, too?' Freda asked.

'This has to be someone else's mistake,' Shirley said.

'Someone else's mistake? You're both forgetting, he escaped on our watch, and you two are the ones so worried that every little detail is perfect,' Mrs Littleton told them.

No one spoke all the way back to the station. Freda grabbed the phone and called security. She told them what was happening and listened. Then she hung up.

'No one has seen hide nor hair of him down there.'

'They were probably playing cards or watching television, I'm sure. It's like guarding a cemetery.'

'What do we do?'

'You know what we do,' Shirley said.

'Your turn to make a call to him,' Freda said.

'Thanks a lot,' Shirley replied. 'How am I going to explain this? And on top of what you just told him about Sutter?'

'Just tell it like it happened,' Mrs Littleton said. 'While we were checking on Mr Sutter, Mr Morris . . .'

'Got up, detached himself from the monitors, which we didn't notice, changed into the janitor's clothes and walked out?' Shirley asked.

'It's what happened, isn't it?' Mrs Littleton said. 'Just stress how long we were with Sutter. Maybe tell him we did try the pads.'

Shirley nodded.

'Yes,' she said. 'That's good. We were in there working on him. That will be our story.'

'Lots of good it will do,' Freda said.

They all stared at the phone as if it were a time bomb.

'There goes my down payment for sure,' Shirley Cole said and then shrugged and made the call.

One

Ceil Morris stepped out of the Starbucks on the corner of her West Side block and casually strolled up the walk toward her apartment building. Other pedestrians flew by her as if she were standing still. She wasn't walking softly and slowly because she was relaxed or uncertain of her direction and destination. She simply couldn't move much faster. She had felt the dull ache in her hip on the right side awaken, grow stronger and pulsate down the back of her leg the moment she had stood up in Starbucks. Her reaction to the pain was more in line with rage than fear. She gritted her teeth and cursed under her breath, panning the lower West Side neighborhood as if she expected to spot some patient assassin who was relentlessly following her and killing her bit by bit, taking his time, slowly poisoning her muscles, her joints, her very blood.

First, it was trouble with two of her upper teeth, both root canal episodes that nearly depleted her relatively small money market account, not to mention the pain and the fatigue that followed as a result of it. Then it was the worst bout of irritable bowel syndrome she had endured her entire fifty-four years, and now it was this hip problem that was tumbling head over heels toward a hip replacement, something she could not afford. Like the other forty-five or so million Americans she had no health insurance. She had no real savings to speak of, just her small money market balance and close to two thousand dollars in cash hidden in her apartment. That was it. She owned no real estate, had no valuable jewelry and absolutely no stocks or bonds.

Endure until you die, she thought. The poor don't fear death as much as the rich. For the poor it's a solution.

She paused to take another deep breath. She could choke to death on her agitation, every moment of reality another bitter pill to swallow. Her sales lady position at Folio, a discount clothing and shoe store, took far more out of her than she received from it. The store was always busy and the lower income customers were just as demanding, and in many cases as downright nasty and arrogant, as the wealthier ones who shopped at Saks or Bergdorf Goodman, not that she had ever worked in either. She had window-shopped there and observed. She was lucky to get the job she had, even though it was only a little above minimum wage and carried no benefits other than a thirty percent discount on anything she wanted to buy at the store.

Like so many women her age, Ceil hadn't prepared herself for economic independence, and after her husband had died, she was shocked to discover how little he had left her. He had even neglected to pay life insurance premiums. She was a struggling widow for more than ten years. Twice she came close to remarrying and both times pulled out just in time when she discovered the first guy was a closet alcoholic and the second had a sex offender record.

An unmarried woman in her mid to late thirties was at a terrible disadvantage these days, she thought, much less someone her age. The eligible bachelors were either rejects from a number of relationships, or in some way ill prepared for a long-term commitment. Once anyone passed the age of twenty in this country, he or she was so embedded in his or her own ways, it was nearly impossible to spell compromise, much less actually achieve it.

To be honest, she, too, had settled into herself. She no longer envisioned sharing anything, even coffee, with a man. He'd want it weaker or he'd want decaf for sure. That's the kind of bad luck she had all her life with men, every man, even her own son.

The worse thing about all this was the fact that sexual pleasure was rapidly becoming a distant memory, and she wasn't all that unattractive either. Her ailments had aged her over the past year or so, but she still held on to a decent figure and a clear complexion. Now that she had gone through the root canal, her teeth weren't as bad as they were for so many women her age. Perhaps she could do more with her hair. She had let it gray. She didn't like the inexpensive color rinses and getting periodic color treatments in a real salon was financially prohibitive. However, it was really the aches and pains that kept her from addressing her appearance. She felt like she was sinking in the muck of self-neglect.

Maybe, this was the feeling we all get before we actually do sink into the ground, she thought. I shouldn't be suffering like this. Damn it all, I shouldn't be suffering at all. She paused to glance back at Starbucks. Something, some sixth sense had urged her to do so. An elderly man, and she meant really elderly, dressed in what looked like a custodian's outfit, had paused when she paused. She blinked at the memory of seeing him outside the café. It appeared as if he were looking in at her, but at the time she imagined he was just looking through the window at the place, fantasizing a frozen mocha or something. What she didn't want to start developing was that paranoia older people took on when they reached the point when they felt vulnerable to anything and everything. She hated the idea that she was one of the so-called older, a card carrying member of the American Association of Retired People, but it was logical to worry. Who made easier and better prey than the older folks, desperate for some hope?

However, that's not going to be me, she thought. I won't fall into any of these traps of age. I refuse to be a day older than I am and, in fact, I want to be and look younger than I am. I'll start working on it again. That's what it was all about these days in America anyway, youth, youth, youth, she thought bitterly.

She continued up the walk mumbling to herself, chanting her determined thoughts until she made the turn toward the entrance of her apartment building, a degenerating brownstone that had once been the proud home of persevering immigrants forging a successful life in this land of opportunity. Why had it never been so for her? She was certainly feeling like a foreigner these days.

At the graffiti-marred entrance she paused and, despite her driving desire not to be paranoid, nervously looked back for the elderly man. She didn't see him. Smiling to herself – and at herself – she shook her head, inserted the key and opened the front door. She paused in the small entryway and tried to remember if she had checked for her mail this morning on the way out. She couldn't recall so she took out the mailbox key and went ahead. There was the usual pile of bills and there were some advertisements stuffed awkwardly by a postman probably annoyed at all the junk mail he had to deliver. At the bottom of the short stack, she saw she had received another letter from her older sister Edith, married and living in Duluth.

The contrast between herself and her sister couldn't have been more stark. Edith had three successful grown children, two boys and a girl, all married with families of their own. The boys were both attorneys and her daughter was a CFO at a major advertising company in Minnesota. Edith's husband owned and still operated a half dozen automobile franchises. They had a real Thanksgiving, inundated with family. They swam warmly through kisses and hugs and felt complete. 'Jingle Bells' never made them feel sad or nostalgic.

She stared at the letter, confident her sister again would be pleading for her to consider coming to live in Duluth where she promised to set her up in decent housing and where she would have family nearby. It wasn't difficult to understand why she avoided doing this. It was a total admission of failure. Not only was her marriage nothing to speak about, but there was Bradley. Her only child hung out there in Halloween imagery. She could imagine his face turned into a mask to frighten people, especially children. To survive with this great disappointment and failure in her life, she convinced not only other people but herself that she was childless. She had borne no fruit in her marriage.

She needed the front door key to get through the second door as well. It was all part of the extra security just recently established with the change of locks, installation of window bars and alarms. She couldn't remember when homes had become more like fortresses, but she certainly felt shut away when she closed the door to her apartment behind her. She fished the key out of her purse again. As she inserted it, she couldn't help voicing a moan because the pain in her hip raged across her lower back as she leaned over to insert the key. Just a small abrupt movement like that could get it to sing, or rather buzz, through her body like a shot of electricity.

She opened the door just as she heard the outside door open. Because of the pain, it took her a moment to turn, but there he was, the elderly gentleman, standing in the doorway.

Something about the look in his eyes, the shape of his face, the features, although wrinkled and aged, stopped her from feeling any panic. It was very, very odd.

'Can I help you?' she asked him.

He started to smile, his lips thinning and whitening to reveal his yellow teeth and dark cavernous mouth. She could easily imagine the halitosis and she actually stepped back, poised to close the second door quickly and lock him out.

'I don't think so, Mom,' he said. 'It's too late.'

Detective Palmer Dorian closed his eyes for a moment to savor the delicious memory of his week with Tracy Anderson in the Dominican Republic. His good friend and attorney Marty Loman was able to get one of his wealthier clients to offer, with a little gentle arm twisting, his villa which came with a maid, cook and swimming pool. Marty's client was developing condos on the island and Marty had done a great deal of work for him, and would do more. It was good to have influential friends. As his mother was fond of saying, 'It's not what you know, but whom you know.' She was a former English teacher so she always got her 'who' and 'whom' right, he thought smiling at the way she would clamp on his father for his incorrect use of 'good' and 'well'.

The contrast between the quiet warmth and tropical sunshine of the Dominican Republic with his claustrophobic life in his lower Westside apartment was truly a culture shock. The people in the Dominican Republic were dirt poor, but exceedingly friendly. They seemed oblivious to their poverty and difficult conditions, in fact. Three times he and Tracy had gotten lost looking for a restaurant and all three times, pedestrians, and one time another driver, literally took them to their destination and were embarrassed to accept money for doing it. Tracy teased him about getting lost.

'Where's that famous psychic intuition you supposedly have, Detective Dorian?' she asked. 'I thought you were the poor man's Charlie Chan.'

'I'm too relaxed here,' he replied. 'It doesn't work without real tension, pressure, a sense of crisis. Whether we find a restaurant or not isn't that critical. As it wouldn't have been to Charlie Chan,' he explained, half-kidding. After all, it sounded logical to him.

'Sure, sure,' she said laughing. 'I couldn't imagine you too relaxed anywhere.'

However, it was true. He was relaxed. For seven glorious days, the grime and blood-dried crust of his day-to-day homicide investigations was blown out of his memory. He didn't feel harried; he had instead this loose, happy demeanor, this sense that every day was beautiful just for them and they could do whatever they wanted. He was sure a good part of his brain had gone into a well-earned rest, especially that part that was continually processing motives and clues. Suspicion, that touch of paranoia he believed all good law enforcement officers must have, was hibernating. All that mattered was his and Tracy's laughter, their affection, their private ecstasy.

It wasn't a honeymoon, but it was as close to one as he thought he would ever get. Unlike most of the women he knew in their late twenties, Tracy Anderson was not at all nervous or concerned about her future. She reeked self-confidence with the redolent power of a ripe onion. Comfortable with her sexuality and her emotions, she never even hinted at the need for any more of a commitment from him. Indeed, he had begun to wonder if she would eventually dump him like a thoroughly squeezed orange and move on with the emotional indifference of changing a channel on a television set.

Somehow, in fact, the three magic words, I love you, weren't uttered by either of them. It was always 'You're great' or 'That was terrific' or simply, 'You make me happy'. It seemed they hadn't even invested emotionally enough in each other to have a bad argument. Contradictions were destined to be shrugged off or even ignored. Nothing seemed that important. Was this the perfect relationship or what?

Mr Big Shot, he told himself, pretending you don't give a damn about settling down and having children, a mortgage and worrying about college tuition. Somewhere, just lying dormant, hibernating with that intuitive power of yours, if you will, is that desire to have something more to care about and work for and die for than yourself. Mr Big Shot. That was what his mother called him these days. That was the extent to how harshly she would ever dare criticize him. His father teased him and called him Our Own Dirty Harry.

No matter how they joked about it, Palmer sensed that his

parents were afraid he would end up alone, hardened and damaged by the daily dosage of ugly, vicious acts of the people he had to investigate and arrest. He had to think like a criminal to catch a criminal and the danger was he would become unattractive as a prospect for a long-term happy relationship, if not physically then emotionally and psychologically, It was truly as if no bath, no cologne, nothing would or could get the stench of the gruesome crimes off him. He seriously wondered if such a thing were true.

His older brother Marcus was in the soda bottling business with his father, married with two children, both girls, ten and eight. Marcus and his wife Charlene were always trying to fix him up with a 'marrying kind of girl'.

'You're like pot smokers,' he told them. 'You're uncomfortable smoking if a non-smoker is in the room, too.'

During a lull, he sat at his desk thinking about all this. Was he too into himself, too self-centered? Was that really what ultimately prevented him from becoming committed to someone else? He was certainly neurotic about his physique, never missing an opportunity to shape and strengthen his muscles and always conscious of his weight? At six feet one, one-hundred and eighty pounds, he was still built like a high-school athlete, rationalizing that his attention to physical stamina and strength was mandatory for anyone in law enforcement. Although the dramatic pursuits through the streets of the city depicted in movies and television were really very rare, as was hand-to-hand combat, he wanted to be ready, as primed for action as a fireman.

Of course, none of that explained his pretty-boy attention to his stylistic clothes and shoes and the attention he gave his light-brown hair. He smiled to himself thinking about Tracy's comment that he spent more time on his appearance than she did.

'It's as though you think you're going to be discovered and put on a magazine cover,' she teased, but quickly admitted she thought he was damn sexy. 'I'd put you on my cover any day.'

Her just saying that made her hot. He closed his eyes and visualized her and when he did so, he released an audible sigh.

'What, are you having a wet dream on the job?' Tucker

Browning asked him as he arrived with some forensic reports they were both supposed to review.

'Not that I know of, but I'll check,' he said and spun around in his seat.

Poof, there goes the Dominican Republic and the image of Tracy in that abbreviate bikini strutting to the side of the pool, the sunlight bouncing off her smile as if she were the one who provided daylight. Maybe for him, she was, he thought. Today was his thirty-first birthday and she had just called to tell him she had made a reservation for them at Rossini's, one of the first places they had gone to together.

'I thought you might have to go to Washington,' he said when she had told him.

'Slipped through it. It's what they call finessing the boss,' she said.

Tracy worked for a Donald Trump clone as a personal assistant and was making triple Palmer's detective's salary. During the two years he had known her, she had even quadrupled his salary with some bonuses. Real estate, business acquisitions, shopping centers were her areas of expertise. She moved her palms over all of it as if the world were one checker board and with a move, a jump here or there, changed people's jobs, homes and lives in general. However, she was about as nonchalant about that as she was about herself. He both admired and resented her for that self-confidence. He wished she needed him more or at least gave him the feeling she did.

'This should lock it up,' Tucker said handing him the DNA results after a quick perusal.

He read the affirmation with glee. They had been investigating the rape and murder of a seventy-two-year-old woman who barely survived on social security living in a subsidized housing development. Clues quickly led them to a young janitor, who looked like he had been hatched from an egg Satan had fertilized on a boring day of sin. Palmer didn't need psychic or even intuitive abilities to suspect him. Guilt lay in the man's eyes like a blood spot in an egg yolk.

'They should all be this easy,' he said waving the paperwork at Tucker.

Tucker Browning leaned back in his chair and pinched his temples with his long, thin spidery fingers. He was ten years older than Palmer and all of those ten additional years were spent in homicide. At six feet four, with dull brown, thin hair and a Lincolnesque sad face, cut with wrinkles so deep they looked like they had been there from birth, Tucker Browning always looked like he was five minutes from retirement or retreat. He was a plodder, a by-the-book soldier who trusted every code and rule he ever had confronted. He depended on them and believed in them the way a scientist might believe in Newton's Law. He was always wary of any diversion which made for dramatic contrast between them because Palmer was always thinking out of the box and eager to forgo procedure. The truth was Palmer's reliance on instinct and intuition was a continual irritation for Tucker, who needed tangible, concrete reasons for anything they did. However, they held on to their partnership and friendship, both recognizing value in the other.

Somehow, however, even though he was in this for the long haul, Palmer didn't see himself as much a career detective as did Tucker. It was as if someday something else would occur. Maybe Tracy wasn't so off the mark imagining he dreamed of being on magazine covers. Perhaps some other more interesting opportunity would waltz into the office and choose him for a partner. Tucker had no such illusions. He accepted himself and his life so completely that he was almost part of the furniture.

'I'll get this over to the chief so he can get it over to the district attorney's office,' Tucker said rising slowly and taking back the paperwork. Lanky, but quick on his feet when he had to be, Tucker spent a smile. He was as thrifty with his happy moments as Silas Marner with his pieces of gold. 'Case closed,' he added.

'Another notch in the belt.'

Tucker nodded and turned just as a uniformed officer was leading Ceil Morris through the office toward their desks. It was clear to both of them that they were the targeted destination.

'Uh oh,' Palmer said. 'Hold your water. The day's not over.'

Tucker paused.

'Excuse me, Detective Browning,' the uniformed officer said to Tucker, 'but Mrs Morris here requested to speak with a homicide detective specifically.'

'Oh? You here to report a murder?' Tucker asked her.

'It's not a murder yet, but it will be soon,' Ceil said.

Tucker's bushy eyebrows lifted and fell. He turned to Palmer. 'This is Detective Palmer Dorian. He's in charge of soon-to-be capital crimes, ma'am. He has a way sometimes of anticipating them,' Tucker added, grateful for the opportunity to kid Palmer about his so-called intuitive powers. He set up a chair for her to sit on and then smiled at Palmer rather impishly before he continued on to make his report.

'Thank you, Sergeant,' Palmer told the uniformed policeman. He pulled himself closer to his desk and opened a pad. 'OK, ma'am, why don't you start at the beginning. Let's begin with your full name and address.'

Ceil moaned and sat slowly, her hand pressed to her hip. 'Terrible arthritis,' she explained and then gave him her full name and address.

'Now then, Mrs Morris, what brings you here today?' Palmer asked calmly.

'My son Bradley killed a man during a robbery at a gas station three years ago,' she began.

Palmer paused in writing and looked up. 'Your son killed a man?'

'Yes sir. The murder was so brutal and unnecessary he was sentenced to life in prison. His victim was a father of three young girls and had suffered an injury in his life that made his right hand nearly worthless, so he was no threat to my son or anyone for that matter. I think my heart shrunk inside my chest when I sat in that courtroom and heard all the grisly details. I can count on the fingers of one hand how many good days I've had since.'

'I see. I'm sorry,' Palmer said. 'But . . .'

'Another inmate killed him in prison six months ago,' she said sharply. 'I arranged for the funeral and buried him. My heart was broken, of course, but I also thought it might be God's justice so I swallowed back my tears and went through the motions, doing what was necessary and praying for his redemption.'

'I see. So you're here because he was murdered in prison. But, that's not a crime going to happen,' Palmer said, really talking more to himself. 'And it's not in our jurisdiction anyway. I'm afraid I don't . . .'

'I mean I thought I buried him,' she continued. 'I saw his body in the funeral parlor briefly. I couldn't look at him long.

The coffin was closed during the service because of the gruesome injury to his head and to his face.'

'Yes, and . . .'

'And I just saw him.'

Palmer smiled and shook his head. 'I'm afraid I don't understand, ma'am. You just saw who? I mean, whom?'

'My son.'

'Who died and whom you buried?'

'Yes.'

'Oh.' Palmer looked toward the chief's office. Tucker, get your ass back here, he thought.

'Only, he was older than I am,' she added.

'Who was older?'

'My son.'

'Your son who died and whom you buried is older than you are,' he repeated as if that was the only way he could hear the words.

'And he's going to die very soon. Maybe he's dead already. That's why I'm here.'

'But you said he was already dead.'

'I said I thought he was.'

Forcing patience down his own throat, Palmer smiled. 'OK, Mrs Morris, then if he wasn't dead and you didn't bury him, who was buried?'

'I don't know who I eventually buried.' She leaned toward him to whisper. 'I suspect when it came time to lower the coffin in the ground, there was no one in it, no body in the box or, if there was a body, it wasn't my son's.' She nodded for emphasis. 'That's what I think.'

Palmer stared at her. She looks normal, he thought. How amazing madness is. Crazy people ought to develop hives on their faces or at least a big lump on their forehead where the madness raged and was stored. Even for him, a trained detective, with good instincts, it was often impossible to determine who was a paranoid schizophrenic or a multiple personality. The madness didn't always take a physical toll on their bodies. In fact, some of the lunatics seemed to grow stronger and look healthier than the so-called sane.

'I'm afraid you're not making much sense, Mrs Morris. Your son can't be older than you are, now can he?' he asked in a soft, calm, but condescending tone.

'I wouldn't have thought so, no,' she admitted. 'Not until today.'

'I see.'

He took solace in the realization that he would have a fun time describing this one to Tracy at dinner later. He didn't often talk about his job. Most of the cases were too gruesome and didn't make for dinner conversation. It was also classical advice to leave the job behind. Those who didn't keep it locked away back at work suffered burnout much earlier in their careers.

'And what,' he asked, pretending to take notes now, 'happened today especially that has changed your mind about all of this?'

'He came to see me.' She looked at her watch. 'Not more than an hour or so ago.'

'Your dead son, who's now older than you, came to see you about an hour or so ago?'

In his way of thinking, if he forced the nutcases to repeat their insane babble, they would realize the craziness and stop themselves.

Mrs Morris just nodded, her expression unchanging, her confidence unflinching. 'Yes, about an hour ago. I first saw him watching me when I was having a latte at Starbucks. I treat myself to one every Wednesday after work, but only on Wednesdays. They're so expensive. He was standing outside looking into the place like one of those homeless people. There are so many and they are so sad. I didn't realize it was him, nor did I think anything of it until I discovered he had followed me.'

'Um,' he said. 'Do you live alone, Mrs Morris?'

'Yes, my husband died a little more than ten years ago and I never remarried. I work at Folio's Department Store,' she added before he could ask. 'Sales.'

'OK. What department?' Now he did write some notes wondering how she could hold down a regular job and be this off-the-wall.

'Lady's lingerie, third floor.'

'I see. Fine. Do you have any immediate family here or close by?'

'I have only an older sister. She's married and lives in Duluth. None of my uncles or aunts are alive and I have not kept in touch with any cousins. I don't know if they're living or dead and they don't know if I am.'

'What is your sister's name?'

'Edith Zucker. Her husband owns automobile franchises – Zucker Auto Park. He's very well known there.'

'And Bradley was your only child?'

'Yes. Sometimes I regret that we had only one child and sometimes I feel blessed I didn't have another. Maybe another would have turned out the same. Actually, we were unable to have another child. We never bothered to find out if it was because of him or me.'

He ignored that. 'Was your sister, other members of your family at your son's funeral?' he asked.

She bit down on her lower lip and looked like she was going to burst into tears now. 'No,' she said. 'The fact is, I didn't tell them what had happened to Bradley until after he was buried, or supposedly buried,' she quickly corrected. 'I've . . . I've been ashamed of it all. My sister never asked about him. Most people . . . most people don't even know I had a child.'

'I see.'

The possibility that she had imagined the death and funeral suddenly occurred to him. He also thought it was possible she imagined having a child in the first place. People like her twirled his imagination as if it were a top.

'Where is this overage son now?'

'I left him back at my apartment. He collapsed before he could tell me much, but he told me enough to make me want to come here right away. Babbled and mumbled, I should say, convincing me he was already in death's grip. If you saw him, you wouldn't think any emergency medical treatment would make any difference at this point anyway.'

'So . . . you didn't call 911 or call for an ambulance or call anyone else, a neighbor, anyone?'

'No, sir. I came here as quickly as I could. Something terrible has happened.'

'People probably do age faster in prison,' he offered.

'Oh, I imagine they do, but don't forget I was told he was dead. I saw his body and I arranged his funeral,' she reminded him and nodded to make sure he understood.

'Yes, you did say all that.' He was hoping she would recant

that part of her story. 'OK,' he said, taking a deep breath like someone who had to go through the pain, 'what's his full name?'

'Bradley Preston Morris. Preston was my husband's name. As I said, he was my only child. He got in with a bad crowd when he was in high school and never seemed to be able to pull himself out of it. It was like stepping into quicksand. Preston gave up on him long before I did, but I'm afraid I failed as well. No matter what your children do or what the circumstances surrounding it are, Detective Dorian, you can't stop blaming yourself. You give birth to him; you raise him; he lives in your home. I don't hold with those people who blame society or others. It was our failure as parents,' she continued. 'We should have done more. Maybe even moved away. That's why I said I'm not unhappy that I had no more children.'

Palmer couldn't help but admire her for her willingness to assume responsibility. It's all driven her nuts, he thought, but he was moved enough to pretend to believe her and at least look like he cared. And he held with her theory about it. He wished more parents would assume responsibility for the acts of their children.

'OK, you say you left your son back in your apartment where he collapsed?'

'Passed out just as he had begun to tell me how he was in some hospital.'

'Hospital.' He leaped on her words. 'So he was ill. Maybe then he just looked a lot older.'

'Oh, he looks a lot older, Detective Dorian. When you see him, I will understand why you won't believe he's my son. But you keep forgetting that I told you he was dead. He was buried. I arranged the funeral.'

'Yes, I keep forgetting,' he muttered.

Tucker was starting back from the chief's office. Palmer smiled to himself thinking about his reaction when this report was summed up for him.

'For now, so that we can deal with this the way we deal with reports, let's just call this man a stranger who came to your apartment. Did he threaten you in any way?'

'Oh no. He was pathetic, very sad.'

'Was there any sign of trauma, violence done to him?'

'No, sir. He looked like anyone's grandfather, great-grand-father, actually. His face was covered with gray stubble, deeply cut wrinkles, his hair thin, his body very fragile, a croak in his voice when he spoke. He looked like he was a hundred years old!' she emphasized just as Tucker stepped up.

'Well now,' Tucker said. 'What do we have here, Detective Dorian?'

Palmer scooped up his notepad and stood. 'Why don't we talk about it on the way over to Mrs Morris' apartment, Detective? This is Detective Browning, ma'am. He forgot to introduce himself before.'

Ceil nodded and stood up. 'Someone's done a terrible, terrible thing,' she told Tucker.

'Well, that's what we're here to prove most of the time, ma'am. This is the place people come to when terrible things have been done.'

'That's exactly why I came,' she replied, without missing a beat.

Palmer smiled at Tucker, who quickly and reluctantly lost his wise ass smirk. He started to raise his arms in protest.

'It looks like she's reporting an unattended death,' Palmer told him before he could question the move. 'Ma'am, please follow us to our automobile,' he added and gestured for Ceil to start down the corridor.

'I thought what she was reporting was an impending murder. Unattended death? What the hell is this?' Tucker whispered.

'That's what we're off to find out, Detective First Class Browning,' Palmer said. 'I'll see to it that she relates her details as we go. I think you'll find it all quite a lot more interesting than this recent easy case.'

'Spare me. I'd rather have easy than interesting.'

'Maybe this is both,' Palmer told him, although his intu-ition was telling him otherwise in broad, strangely alarming strokes.

It would be interesting but not easy.

Nevertheless, he checked his watch and thought if he could get this over with within two hours, he wouldn't have any problem getting ready for dinner with Tracy.

That, more than anything, drove him to move it along.

Two

S imon Oakland stood looking out of the ten-story high
window of his office which overlooked the small pond
and a few acres of what were now richly green oak, hemlock
and birch trees co-habiting in that part of the New York Catskill
mountain forest that had been spared. On the other side and
to the north and south of it were two similar tract housing
developments. From this height, because of their dull silvery
tiled roofs, they looked like gray mold spreading a disease
over the landscape. People from New York City looking for
second-bedroom homes bought most of the houses. The mass-
produced structures were inexpensive enough to enable truly
middle class income people to afford them and get the sense
that they were entering territory inhabited only by the very
wealthy: a multi-home portfolio.

Simon was sure that when they talked about their country
homes, they left out the fact that the homes were tract houses
in a development. This was far from the romantic image of
'my home in the country'. These houses were built with
synthetic materials, standardized appliances and fixtures, and
set on the minimum permitted lot sizes with uniform land-
scaping, driveways and sidewalks. The only thing individual
about each of the homes was the number on the front to
indicate the address. Come home drunk one night and you
could enter the wrong life, he thought and laughed to himself
imagining it.

But these people were happy in these houses. Ours is an
economy with a foundation consisting of illusions, he thought,
and yet how could he fault them for wanting the illusion?
They had theirs and he had his.

He clutched his hands behind his back and rocked gently
on his small feet. At five feet three, he barely broke out of
children's sizes, whether it was his shoes, just a six, or his

pants and shirts. To avoid the embarrassment, he had almost everything he wore custom made and only occasionally picked up a coat or a pair of shoes at a store. He wasn't much of a shopper anyway. The fact was he hated mingling with the masses, as he called it. He could count on the fingers of one hand how many times he had been to a shopping mall. He never went to a movie or to the theater anymore, and his maid and cook, Mrs Goodman, bought all of his groceries and house needs. The house had been bought for him and she had been hired for him by Mr Dover's corporation, which provided for his medical and dental needs as well.

Simon never saw a tax form, a bill or any sort of business correspondence whatsoever now. Over the past four years, he had only his work with which to concern himself. He merely had to mention a worry or a concern and it was immediately addressed. He was sure kings never lived better or had more attention. He had his own chauffeur and the use of Mr Dover's private jet whenever he was required to travel or wanted to, not that he had wanted to very much these last four years. He was a workaholic who rarely left the compound.

What motivated him and kept him centered and satisfied with his solitary life was his belief that what he was doing would have as much influence on human history as the discovery of electricity or maybe even the wheel. Some day, not now of course, but some day, his name would be in text-books alongside the Edisons and the Einsteins. There was even the chance that before he died, he would be awarded the Nobel prize or something equivalent. Leaders of all sorts of governments would heap medals and awards on him. He would be an international celebrity. He even harbored the hope that his work and his creations would be baptized the Oakland Method, or some such title. Why not? The British named all vacuum cleaners Hoovers, and what he was doing was not ten times more important; it was closer to a million times more important.

He rocked on his feet again and squeezed his hands, a nervous action that he recognized as such but nevertheless performed. Normally, he was about as calm and contented a man as could ever be, but when he was told to be in his office for a phone call from Mr Dover, he felt his quickened heart-beat, a surge of blood to his face and an electric chill in his spine. It was like getting a phone call from God, a communication not only over long distances, but over time itself.

He knew what it was about, knew that Mr Dover had been told what had occurred on the Final Stage floor and probably told before he had been told. Those employees were more loyal to him. It was Dover's MO to staff the program with people dependant more on him than on Simon. He was keenly aware that there were spies everywhere. He wouldn't even trust Mrs Goodman. Perhaps she was the least trustworthy of all in fact because she was directly involved in his personal life.

But, this was all worth the price. Look at what he had, what he could do. It was only Mr Dover who commanded this much fear and respect from him anyway. Because of his knowledge, skill and creativity, he lorded over most other men much taller and bigger than he was, and even wealthier and more politically powerful and connected. None of them wanted to be on his wrong side or in any way even annoy him. They practically bowed when they left him and kept their eyes down as if to look directly at him was an affront and punishable by death.

And he did have his own spies and loyal associates. His hand-picked assistant, Larry Hoffman, had called to warn him that the nurses on the Final Stage floor had informed Mr Dover about Bradley Morris' escape, just minutes after they had informed him of Sutter's death.

He heard the phone ring and turned, first just looking at it as if he really had a choice about answering it. What was it Sartre had written about the power of Existentialism? A man caught in an overpowering current and carried downstream could still hold on to his essence, his self-meaning by deciding to swim faster than the current. He still invoked choice and to exist was to choose.

Simon pondered lifting the receiver slowly or quickly, pausing deliberately and then saying hello or lunging for the receiver and answering quickly, even before the ear piece reached his ear. He opted for the first choice and casually lifted the receiver and didn't speak until he was seated behind his oversize dark-cherry desk. His chair elevated him, but to anyone else the desk looked like it enveloped him and he was sinking in the wood. He didn't care. Everything that touched him and he touched grew larger, longer, wider because of him.

'Simon Oakland,' he said even though he knew exactly who was calling.

'This is a very, very serious glitch, Simon,' Mr Dover said without any introduction or small talk.

'Glitch?' What kind of a word was *glitch*?

'You know what I mean. How could Bradley Morris have the strength and mind to escape your clinic? I thought he was another one in his final days, another overly ripe tomato, as you put it to me once.'

Simon was silent, but his brain was whacking formulas and thoughts like balls on a racket ball court.

'I said more than that, Mr Dover. I did say we have to take genetics into consideration. It's why some people live to be in their nineties even though they smoke and don't exercise regularly. Remember George Burns?'

'Don't be condescending, Simon. This is not acceptable and you know it,' Mr Dover shouted, his voice snapping like a whip through the receiver. Simon actually lifted it from his ear and rubbed his lobe.

'I'm working on it, sir. I'm back to the drawing board and reviewing my findings,' he said quickly. 'I was on it the moment I heard from Dr Hoffman and ever since. I've stopped working only to take your call.'

'I'm putting the other volunteers on indefinite hold until I hear back from you, Simon. There could be other problems because of this. This is not good.'

'You don't have to do that, sir. I'm sure this relates only to this one specimen. The program will be fine,' Simon assured him, some panic now slipping into his voice. Could he lose it all, everything when he was this close?

'Don't tell me what I have to do and not do, Simon. This is not good,' Mr Dover said with more firmness. 'The man is still out there somewhere. You understand what that means for all of us, especially for you? It's too soon for anyone to know anything or ask any questions.'

'Yes, of course, sir,' he said.

'I have critical clean-up to arrange and that isn't easy or pleasant for me. I have to ask for favors from people I would rather were in debt to me.'

'I understand.'

'I'm not sure you do. You're too aloof. My God, man, you don't even know how to write a check properly. Find a solution to this glitch, Simon, and quickly or we'll have to pack up the whole thing and disappear into the woodwork. That includes you. You won't even live in your mother's memory,' he threatened.

He wanted to say he probably never did anyway. His mother never understood him and secretly hoped babies were accidentally exchanged in the nursery. She voiced that idea. His physical resemblance both to her and his father was so slight she actually had him wondering.

'I will be on it day and night until it's solved, Mr Dover. I promise.'

The phone went dead; the receiver felt like a bird dying in his hand. When he was a little boy, he had found a small bird with a broken wing and held it and was amazed at how fragile were its bones and how easily he could squeeze the life out of it. It gave him the idea that life was something we sponged up, all living things sponged up, and when death came along, all he had to do was squeeze the sponge and life came seeping out.

He pressed the intercom.

'Miss Pearson,' his nurse on duty at the clinic announced. There were two nurses, splitting shifts and he always forgot which ones were on duty.

'Prepare number five. I need to give our specimen another treatment,' he told her. 'Run another blood work up immediately on the specimen as well,' he added.

She didn't respond so much as grunt. He knew his referring to another human being as a 'specimen' struck a discordant note with Miss Pearson as it did with Mrs Randolph, his other nurse assistant, even though neither of them would dare say anything to him. He knew they complained at times to Larry Hoffman, however. When one or the other looked like she might make a comment to him, he challenged her by asking, 'Is anything wrong?'

Of course each quickly shook her head.

He enjoyed teasing women. He always had, maybe because he felt none would ever look at him with any sexual interest. Once he achieved his goals here, succeeded beyond a doubt, he would be something akin to a rock star, he thought. Then they would pay attention to him and want to be in his bed.

Was that what motivated him to do all this in the first place? What a disappointing realization that would be if he discovered that he was motivated by the same urges and needs as any other man, and be just another one of those pebbles on the beach.

After all this, what could be more devastating than to learn he was mortal after all?

And maybe, just another specimen.

Tucker Browning didn't say a word. He listened and held his forward gaze with such firmness it was as if he was terrified of moving his head to either side. Ceil Morris sat in the rear and simply added, 'That's right,' whenever Palmer reconfirmed a part of the story she had told him.

'Well now,' Palmer said as they pulled to the curb in front of Ceil Morris' brownstone. 'Here we are, Mrs Morris.'

He parked and then glanced at Tucker who finally moved himself to reach for the door handle, shaking his head slightly as he did so. They all got out and the two men then silently followed Ceil Morris to her building entrance. She began to relate the events again as she inserted her door key.

'I stopped to check my mailbox as I always do when I return from work. For some reason, I wasn't sure if I had checked it this morning. Isn't that strange?' she asked them, turning back before she searched for the key. 'Isn't it strange how our memories play tricks on us when we get a little older? You seem to forget the simplest things.'

'Yes, our memories do play tricks on us,' Tucker said dryly.

'I do have to confess that I was more than a little nervous because I was afraid he was following me. I sensed it. You can sense things sometimes.'

'Yes, you can,' Tucker said and smiled at Palmer.

'I suppose that could explain my confusion as well. Anyway, he wasn't anywhere in sight so I entered the building just like this,' she said opening the door and stepping into the entryway.

'The woman is so far off the wall, she's in another state, if not another country,' Tucker whispered to Palmer and then held the door for him. He entered and Ceil paused to insert her mail key in the mailbox.

'I thought you already got your mail, Mrs Morris,' Tucker said.

'Oh, I did, but I just thought I should do everything the same way so you get a complete picture.'

'Yes,' Tucker said smiling. 'A complete picture. Thank you. Yes.'

She opened and closed the mailbox.

'Then I opened the inside door, paused and looked back because I heard the entrance door open.'

'But how could that be?' Palmer asked quickly. 'You need a key to open the entrance door. You just used it.'

'Oh. Yes. I must have not let it close all the way. It does that often. You have to actually remember to turn around and push it closed. Very good, Detective Dorian.'

'Yes, very good, Detective Dorian,' Tucker said.

Palmer nudged him with his elbow.

'Anyway, there he was standing in the doorway. I wasn't afraid of him. He looked too old to hurt anyone but himself and even that would be difficult for him, I thought. I asked him if I could help him and he said, "I don't think so, Mom. It's too late." That's what he said.'

'He definitely said "Mom"?' Palmer asked her.

'Absolutely. It threw me back and I know I was just standing there with my mouth wide open. I could see he was starting to cry, too. "Yes, it's me, Mom," he said. "It's Bradley." Of course, I couldn't believe it and I shook my head. 'You can't be my son,' I said. 'My son couldn't be as old as you and anyway, my son is dead. I saw his body. I was at his funeral. This is not very funny.'

'"I'm your son all right," he insisted and then he turned to show me the pear-shaped birthmark on the right side of his neck. My husband used to tease him when he was little and tell him I had eaten a pear before giving birth to him.'

'Cute,' Tucker said.

'Yes. Anyway, when I saw it, I thought my legs would give out on me. Instead, it was he who faltered, steadied himself against the wall, closed and opened his eyes, and pleaded for me to get him into my apartment. He was very, very thirsty, too.

'At this point I didn't know what to do or say, so I stepped back and held the door for him. He came through and when we got to the elevator, he put his arm around my shoulders and I was basically holding him up. He looked asleep by the time I inserted the key into my apartment door. I led him in and he collapsed on the sofa. His head was back and his eyes were closed.

"'Are you all right?" I asked him. His eyelids fluttered. "Water, please, Mom," he said and I hurried to get him a glass of water. I had to feed it to him. "How can you be my son?" I asked him. "I am," he said. "You've got a scar on your right side over your ribs where you fell when you were a little girl. You fell off playground monkey bars. Your rib was fractured."

"'Oh, my God," I said. How would he know that? That's not something I told anyone outside the family.

"'I'm going to die very soon. I'm not sure how I managed to escape and get here under my own steam," he told me.'"

She stepped into the elevator and pushed three. The doors closed. Tucker took a deep breath.

'Escape from where?' Tucker asked. 'What did he mean by that?'

'I don't know. He fell into a deep sleep, maybe a coma. I couldn't wake him to ask him anything else.'

'And then you left him in your apartment?'

'Dying,' she said. 'Dying. That's why I rushed out. I wanted to see someone from homicide. Someone has done something terrible to my son.'

The elevator doors opened and they followed her to her apartment door. She took a very deep breath, crossed herself and then opened the door.

They stepped in with her and looked at the sofa.

There was no one there.

'Where is he?' she asked. 'He must have gotten up.'

'I thought you said he fell into a coma,' Tucker reminded her.

'Yes, he did. I don't understand.'

She hurried through the apartment, checking the bedroom, the kitchen and the bathroom. Both Tucker and Palmer stood there waiting.

'Well?' Tucker asked.

'He's not here,' she said. 'I don't see how he got himself up and left.'

'Is anything missing, Mrs Morris?' Tucker asked in a very tired sounding tone.

'Missing?'

'Check, please,' Palmer said. She stared a moment and then turned and went back into the bedroom.

'*Da da da da, da da da da,*' Tucker sang under his breath, imitating the old *The Twilight Zone* theme.

When Ceil Morris came back to the living room, her face was pale and she was wringing her hands.

'Well?' Tucker asked.

'My money.'

'Your money? What about it?'

'Gone?' Palmer asked her.

'Yes,' she said. 'Money I kept in a dresser drawer is gone,' she said, her face crumbling.

'How much?' Tucker asked.

'Nearly . . .' She paused, choking on the number. 'Two thousand dollars. All my extra money.'

'Son of a bitch,' Palmer said. 'What gimmick won't they think of next to take advantage of people?' He almost said older people, but stopped himself. Nevertheless, she saw it in his face and his eyes.

'How could that be his gimmick? How could he do such a thing?' Ceil asked them.

'Once a thief always a thief,' Tucker said. 'Age doesn't mean anything when it comes to a person's nature.'

She looked up sharply. 'I don't mean his just being older. What I meant,' she said, 'is I'm not surprised he's still a thief, but my own son robbing from me.' Before either Tucker or Palmer could speak, she added, 'It was my son. Actually,' she said lowering her eyes, 'if I want to be honest, I'd have to admit he was very definitely capable of it.' She sank to the sofa with her tone of confession. 'I'm afraid he has done it before. It was what turned my husband against him so much.'

'Mrs Morris,' Tucker began, 'anyone left alone in your apartment like that would look around, find what to take, especially money. Just because you were robbed here doesn't mean it's your son.'

'Oh no, it was my son for sure. Who else would know where I kept my money?'

'Why? Where did you keep it, Mrs Morris?' Palmer asked.

'In an empty Tampax box under a pair of panties at the bottom of a drawer. That's an unusual hiding place, isn't it?'

'Very,' Palmer said.

'A man wouldn't normally open a box of Tampax to search for money,' she said.

'Just a lucky hit, I guess,' Tucker said. 'We'll make a report to the detectives who handle these sort of crimes, ma'am,' he added, ignoring all of her references to the thief being her son.

Who returned from the dead to rob her!

She looked at the floor and shook her head. 'I know you don't believe me. I can understand, but you didn't see it,' she said. 'You didn't see the birthmark or hear what he said. Besides, a mother knows her child.' She looked up sharply at Palmer. 'No matter what, a mother knows her child. I'm not crazy.'

'No one said you were, ma'am,' Tucker said. Palmer continued to stare at her. 'There's some logical explanation for it all.'

'Are you going to be all right?' he asked.

'What? Oh. Yes.'

'Someone will call you and come see you from the police station, Mrs Morris. We'll see to it personally,' he said.

She nodded and stared again at the floor. 'He never called me Mother or Ma. He always called me Mom. Even when he was a little boy. He didn't say Mommy. He always said Mom.'

She looked up at them, her eyes so full of tears, they looked as if they were made of glass.

'He knew where I kept my money, how I hid it. He used to laugh at me, and there was that other time. I told you ... when my husband got so enraged.'

She was babbling now.

'Someone will contact you,' Tucker emphasized. He was obviously uncomfortable in her presence. He reached for the door. 'Palmer?' he said.

Palmer hesitated and then dug into his pocket and produced his card.

'If you think of something else for us, Mrs Morris, or just want to talk about it some more, here's my card.' He took out his pen and wrote something on the back. 'My home number is here as well.'

She looked up gratefully and took it. 'Thank you, Detective Dorian,' she said.

'Palmer,' Tucker said from the door.

Palmer joined him, but looked back at her once before closing the door. She looked pathetic, lost, stunned, aging herself right before his eyes.

Neither of them spoke until they were in the elevator.

'One for the books,' Tucker said. 'Robbed by a dead son, hiding money in a box of Tampax . . .'

Palmer was pensive.

'Why the hell did you give her your home number?'

Palmer didn't respond. Tucker stopped walking.

'All right, what's bothering you, Palmer? And don't deny that something is. I can see that crystal-ball mind of yours spinning.'

Palmer waited until the elevator door opened and then he turned to him. 'I believe her,' he said. 'Don't ask me why, but I believe her.'

Tucker stopped walking and watched him go to the entrance. Then he shook his head and followed. 'How or why in hell would you believe that story, Palmer? Enlighten me, will ya?'

'It's just an instinctive feeling . . . that mother thing.'

'So, what, are you a mother too now?'

'No, but she was right about a mother always knowing her own child,' Palmer insisted. 'Mother's do have an uncanny ability to recognize their own children, even years and years later. You know that from some of the stories about missing kids who turn up ten, even twenty years later.'

'A mother in her right mind, Palmer. Jesus. I'll do you a favor. I'll take care of this. You go prepare for your special birthday date and forget it, will ya.'

Palmer nodded.

'I mean it, stupid. If you keep thinking about it, you'll go as crazy as she is. It's not brain surgery. This woman lives alone, battles to survive, probably bathes in paranoia and is reaching the end of the line. Maybe she wasn't even robbed. We didn't go look.'

'Huh? No, she was robbed.'

'Right. She was robbed. I'll give it to Wizner. You can check in with him after he does his preliminaries, OK?'

'Yes,' Palmer said and got into the car.

'I can't believe you gave her your home number,' Tucker repeated.

They drove back to the precinct quietly.

'OK, here's a theory,' Tucker said when they pulled into the lot. 'The old bastard who followed her from Starbucks knew her son in prison and knew about the birthmark. He put one on artificially to throw her into a tizzy and get into her place. He also knew about her scar, that story about her falling in a playground. Well?'

Palmer nodded. 'Could be, I suppose.'

'No, Palmer, not could be. Was or is,' Tucker said getting out. 'Oh,' he added holding the door open. He looked in. 'Happy birthday.' He reached into his pocket and threw a small gift box to him.

'What's this?'

'A token of my appreciation that you're getting older,' Tucker said and closed the door.

Palmer opened it to find a very attractive, antique pocket watch. There was even an inscription inside: *Every minute counts. Your buddy, Tucker.*

Palmer smiled and looked as his partner entered the precinct. After hearing Ceil Morris' story, nothing rang truer, he thought.

Then he focused his thoughts on Tracy and put Mrs Morris and, for now, the strange story out of sight and out of mind.

He would not burn out quickly.

He would survive.

Three

Even though as a kid he had done it, he hated robbing his own mother, especially when he saw how she was living. How she was surviving was more like it. He hadn't seen her for years before he had been arrested and put on trial. She looked pathetic then, but even more so now with her hair almost completely gray, her face so thin and her eyes so vacant. Despite his fatigue, he almost moved faster than she did. For a moment he felt sorrier for her than he did for himself.

However, he saw no other solution, but to steal her money. He needed money to continue and he knew he couldn't explain all of it in a way she would understand. She certainly wouldn't willingly give him the money. What she even more certainly wouldn't understand or sympathize with was his driving need for revenge, but what else could he do? Retreat to an old-age home and die?

You could have died there with her at least, he told himself.

What sort of a choice was that?

He was always like this, imagining arguments and getting himself all worked up and enraged before a word was spoken. While he was growing up, it happened too often in relation to his mother and certainly his father. He would go to sleep dreaming of smashing their faces with a rock or a frying pan to shut them up.

It amazed him how his mother hadn't changed in some ways. She still kept way more cash than was necessary or prudent in a Tampax box under her panties in the bottom dresser drawer. She was always thinking about being prepared. Something terrible would happen and not having actual money in hand would prove to be disastrous. Credit cards and banks would fail.

But look where she hid it. Somehow, she harbored the belief that someone robbing her wouldn't look in a Tampax box under panties. It was too indecent. From where did she draw these favourable conclusions about human nature, from which well of optimism to think that a thief would have some inhibition or reluctance to look in the box after he had pealed away a piece of underwear in his search for booty?

All his life he had equated kindness and trust with weakness. What other lesson did nature teach so clearly and repeatedly? What other lesson did human history teach so clearly and repeatedly? Expect the worse from people and you'll never be disappointed, was his motto. His immediate problem existed because he hadn't followed that rule to the letter and now he was suffering because of it. He almost blamed himself for the mess he was in as much as he did them.

Them, he thought. They were a group that consisted of lawyers, a priest, scientists and, of course, men of power, wealthy, influential pullers of the strings. Soon, he would be the one pulling their strings or wrapping the strings around their throats.

They had tricked him, used him. They didn't play fair. They weren't embezzling money; they were embezzling life.

There seemed to be no other purpose for his life now than the quest for vengeance. In the condition he was in, what other ambition could he entertain even though he was free? Travel? Meet beautiful women? Accumulate a fortune? None of that was within his grasp or mattered anymore.

Vengeance, on the other hand, would bring a deep sense of satisfaction. In that lay the only hope of once again experiencing happiness and pleasure. There was never anything as delicious as tasting revenge, doling out pain and disappointment to those who had doled it out to him, no matter what their justifications or reasons. There was no higher law than the law that protected his own safety and pleasure. The Bible, the commandments, all those sermons and rules for behaving made absolutely no sense. Churches supported wars and accumulated great wealth; everyone believed God was on his side. When you got right down to it, it was all a matter of convenience, so why not do everything to make things convenient for yourself?

There was, however, one other small hope. He tried to keep it buried under his darker thoughts because it probably would bring him only greater disappointment if he gave it some credence and it turned out to be false hope. However, it was difficult to keep it down. It was like a bubble that found ways to pop up on the surface of the water. It slipped around and under thoughts until it was out there, impossible to deny.

If they could do this, maybe they could reverse it. Maybe they could correct it. Maybe they could take it back. He remembered when he was a young boy, an unadulterated bully, how he could twist some poor sucker's arm or squeeze his balls until he took something back. He not only had them take back nasty words, he had them take back nasty looks. 'Smile and compliment me or I'll burst out your eardrums.'

Lording it over those weaker than him gave him a godlike sense of control and power. He ruled the world, or at least his immediate world. Those who did his bidding or clung to his shadow for protection would make sacrifices, betray their mothers, give up their treasures just to keep him on their side.

Maybe this wasn't such a hopeless ambition, an impossible goal. Maybe he would find a way to twist their arms. That, with the energy coming from his drive for vengeance, renewed him, resuscitated him, sent him charging ahead. He was surprised and grateful for this small turnaround. If only he had enough time, he thought, and wondered if within him, there was an hourglass dripping his seconds, his minutes, his hours, his days, dripping them into some dark hole. Like a sailor tied to an anchor whose rope had been twisted around his ankle, he would follow it down, screaming, waving his arms in vain.

Did he have enough time? Damn it, couldn't he stop the clock?

He looked down the street at a parked taxicab. The driver was smoking a cigarette, taking a break. Could he make it to the cab? And if he did, could he make it to the end of the ride? And if he did, could he make it into the building? Every step, every immediate goal of this journey would be in question, would be another crisis.

His breath was short; his legs wouldn't go much faster, and the aches and pains wouldn't dissipate, but somehow, because he had come this far, because he had surprised himself, he had regained the confidence he needed. He prided himself on not believing in anything but himself, and once again, at least for now, he could do that.

They had taken it away, but it was coming back.

Maybe there was an angry God after all, and maybe, just maybe, he wasn't as angry at him as he was at them. He didn't care if he was being so used by this angry God, exploited. In fact, he welcomed it. 'Yes, use me,' he muttered as he walked. 'Use me, use me.' As long as we have the same goal in mind, he thought, I'll pay the toll and say a prayer, even two. I'll even light a candle.

It made him smile and that was something he thought he would never again do.

Already, he was ahead. Surely, this meant he would succeed.

He banged his closed fist on the taxicab window, surprised at the strength he showed.

'I'm off,' the driver said barely turning to look at him. 'Taking a break. Find another cab.'

He opened the rear door and got in anyway.

'Hey,' the driver said. 'Didn't you hear me, old timer? I'm not on duty.'

He slipped out a knife he had taken from his mother's kitchen and put it up to the driver's neck. 'Drive,' he said, 'or die. The choice is yours and it might be the last one you make, so think carefully.'

There wasn't even a pause. The driver started the engine, put it in drive, and pulled away from the curb.

'Where we going?' he asked, hovering over the steering wheel to keep his throat more protected.

'Back,' Bradley Preston Morris said. 'We're going back.'

'Back? Back where?' the cab driver asked, glancing up at the rear-view mirror.

Bradley's eyes picked up the headlights of oncoming cars and glowed like a cat's. 'Back,' Bradley said in a hoarse whisper. 'Back to where it all began.'

'How disgusting,' Tracy said after Palmer had described the events involving Ceil Morris. Despite the promise he had made to himself after all on his way to pick her up, he couldn't put it out of mind and besides, she saw how distracted he was. She was keen at reading him. There was no sense denying.

'At least she wasn't physically harmed,' he said, thinking about the case he and Tucker had just closed.

'Yes, but somehow, you don't think of elderly people

becoming or remaining thieves while they're on social security. Is this guy the oldest criminal you've come across, you think?'

Palmer loved how animated and excited she could become. Everything seemed to move on her face, but in an adorable way. Her nose twitched slightly like a rabbit's might. Her lips stretched and thinned exploding that dimple in her right cheek. Her eyes widened and brightened with her eyebrows looking as if they were lifting off and, most unusual, her earlobes, tiny and soft, inviting a lover's nibble, quivered, too.

'If I take her word for it, her description of the guy, yes.'

'What a scam.' She sipped her Grey Goose Cosmopolitan and thought a moment. 'I think I'm with you and not with Tucker on this one.'

'Meaning?'

'It can't simply be an old cell mate from prison. Something persuaded her to believe this was her son and it wasn't just the birthmark and a story about some scar. There had to be more, a connection she made with his eyes, his . . . essence, if you like.'

'I know what I said, but Tucker's not wrong, Tracy, To believe that, we have to believe her son aged at least twice as quickly as she has, if not faster.'

'People age under stress.'

'Not like that, like the way she's describing him. No, there has to be another explanation.'

'Hmm. I guess you're right. I'm being too romantic about a mother recognizing her own. She nodded and then smiled. 'Maybe he's a relative she never knew.'

'Maybe.'

'Your work is so much more interesting than mine.'

He laughed. 'That's the first time I ever heard you say that.'

'Well, it is. I crunch numbers, study markets, demographics and meet with people whose most exciting and interesting experience is finding a loophole in a zoning ordinance.'

He laughed harder and then looked at the menu. 'I'm going for the lobster dish,' he said. 'Screw the cost. You're paying.'

'I don't expect that to be all you're screwing tonight,' she teased and blew the fugitive strands of her dark-brown hair away from her cheek. Her hair otherwise fell straight, shoulder-length, soft, rich. It flowed like some liquid jewel around her face.

She belongs in a television commercial, he thought and then, No, I don't want to share her with that many people, men.

Everything she did was sexy to him, even the way she wove her fingers around the stem of her cocktail glass, keeping the tip of her pinky slightly up. He had never paid as much attention to the details of a woman as he did to her. No sense fooling himself any longer or denying it, he thought. *I'm falling head first in love with her.* However, he was afraid of being the first one to express it, absolutely terrified of committing too much, going out too far on that proverbial limb and being rejected and dropped on to the hard surface of cold reality, with her saying something like, 'I thought we were both just out for a good time, neither of us ready to get tangled in the complications of a serious relationship, especially marriage. God forbid marriage.'

The net result would be she would start looking for an exit strategy. He did not know how he had gotten to the point where the woman he was with had so much more control of their relationship than he had, but there it was. Despite his cool, James Bond facade, he was once again a starry-eyed teenager.

'Why Tracy Andersen, how you talk. One would think you were a liberated woman.'

She laughed and turned to the waiter to give him the same entrée order.

'Can't let me outspend you?' he teased.

'Not on my dime, no.'

There was a singer tonight at the restaurant doing romantic Italian songs. With the good food, the wine and now the music, it was heading toward the best birthday dinner he had ever had, excluding the one where he was given his first set of car keys, of course. When he told her that, she smiled, but she didn't laugh or turn it into another joke. She fixed those cerulean eyes on him and softened every hard place in his body. He thought he might just pour out over the table into her hands and let her mold him into anything she wanted.

Afterward, strangely mute, but speaking more with a touch, a kiss, a smile, they went to his apartment. She was a little coy at first. It was as if this were the first time they had ever decided to sleep together. He had the feeling that she was giving herself to him in a deeper, more complex and complete way. Dare he think commitment?

She was the first to say it, mention the word 'love' and then immediately explained why she had been hitherto reluctant to do so. 'People use it too freely,' she explained. 'It's almost automatic, a tag on to a goodbye: I love you. The listener feels obligated to return a "I love you", too. I've always had this sense that people who said it or needed it said were insecure, and if there is one thing I would hate being or even be thought of being, it's insecure, naked.'

'You just talked me out of saying it,' he replied and she punched him playfully on the shoulder. Then he got serious. 'Tracy, if there is one person with whom I don't fear being naked, it's you.'

'That's close,' she decided.

'I don't know where we're going, but I'd be a helluva fool to think of this as dead-ended. I can't imagine anything better.'

'Closer,' she said. 'On second thought, Detective, you have the right to remain silent.'

'Too late. I love you,' he told her and they kissed and made love until they were both exhausted. They fell asleep within minutes of each other, neither able to say which one had dropped off first.

The sound of his phone seemed to come from the end of a tunnel. She had to wake him to tell him he wasn't dreaming it. It was only six fifteen.

'Dorian,' he managed and cleared his throat.

'Now it's ours,' Tucker said.

'What's ours?'

'The case. We don't simply have a senior citizen thief. We have a senior citizen killer. I've been on it for a few hours.'

'Why didn't you call me?'

'Figured I'd give you another birthday present. Was I right?'

'Yes, thanks. Who'd he do?'

'Taxi driver. Witness saw him get out of the cab and saw the driver fall face forward on to his steering wheel.'

'How do you know it's our senior citizen?'

'Description fits . . . the coveralls . . . how old he looked. How many men that old looking like that are out there robbing old ladies and knocking off taxi drivers?'

'Anything else . . . anything in the cab?'

'Forensics on it, but I don't hold up high hopes.'

'Door handle might give up something. His prints would be most recent.'

'Guess what?'

'He wiped it?'

'See, you do have powers of perception,' Tucker kidded.

He shifted his gaze toward Tracy who was propping herself up on her left elbow and staring at him, her eyes full of questions.

'I'll dress and meet you for breakfast,' he told Tucker.

'Maybe we'll have to go back to talk to the crazy lady. See if there's anything else she remembers that might help.'

'Maybe she's not so crazy.'

'No. It's the rest of us,' Tucker said and hung up.

Palmer hung up and lowered his head back to the pillow.

'What? Is it that case? The senior citizen case?'

He nodded.

'Well,' she said shaking him. He looked at her. Her eyes widened. 'What?'

'It appears the same old guy killed a taxi driver.'

'Killed?'

'Yeah.'

'Oh, how dreadful. But he didn't kill the woman claiming to be his mother, did he? What's her name?'

'Ceil Morris.'

'Yes. He didn't harm her except to rob her.'

'The way she described him, he couldn't harm a fly. Maybe he needed his Geritol first or something.'

'Wow.' She fell back to her pillow. 'I told you. Your work is far more interesting than mine.'

'In this case, I'm with Tucker. I'd rather be bored.'

'OK, here's my theory,' she said, sitting up again and letting the blanket fall to her waist. How did she expect him to hear a word? 'Stop it,' she said slapping him playfully when she saw his eyes widen and a little smirk appear through his lips. She pulled the blanket back up and over her breasts. 'Are you listening or not?'

'I am now.'

'It's her son but he's wearing make-up, that's all. There was some mix-up in the prison. He's out and he's wearing make-up to make himself look so old.'

He nodded. 'Yeah, that makes some sense if you believe

they somehow confused identities in a maximum security prison. Highly unlikely, Tracy, and besides, his mother saw him before he was buried. She made the arrangements for the funeral and the burial.'

'Did she?'

'Yes. She said that,' he told her.

'Was it a big funeral?'

'No. She told none of her relatives. She has only a sister and the sister's family.'

'So only she saw him in the casket?'

'Yeah, so?'

'Maybe he wasn't really dead, Palmer. People can make people look like they're dead, can't they? You can be fooled. Especially an overwrought mother.'

'Yeah, but that makes even less sense, Tracy. Why would the prison authority do all that to release a felon? These are not wealthy people. Nobody could buy any favors.'

'I don't know. I don't have all the answers.'

'Tracy, why would her son disguise himself and then tell her he's her son?'

'Because he knew no one would believe her and he wanted to get into her apartment and steal her money,' she fired back.

He shrugged. 'Still doesn't explain how he got out, Tracy. It's too much of a stretch to claim mistaken identity and what you're suggesting is too involved. All sorts of people in authority would have had to be in on it.'

She thought a moment and nodded. 'I guess you're right. It doesn't make any sense. Wow.'

'Yeah, wow.'

'You have no ideas, nothing. Even intuition?'

He shook his head.

She poked him in the chest with a stiff right forefinger and held it there. 'You'd better keep me in the loop on this one, Detective Palmer Dorian, and none of that junk about not bringing the work home with you.'

'Yes, ma'am, but I gotta go,' he said and swung himself off the bed. When he looked back at her, he saw her smiling at his naked butt. It stirred the old juices. 'Well, maybe I can be a little late. Who needs breakfast when I have a full meal here?' he added.

She laughed as he crawled back under the blanket. He

glanced at the window before he embraced her. Morning sunshine sliced through the darkness like a razor, cutting around skyscrapers and finding its way toward the shadows that had thought themselves invulnerable. Like the great beast it was, the city began to stir. Lights went on, traffic increased, noise seemed to rise out of the sidewalks. The images hovered at the rim of Palmer's sexual thoughts. He shook them off like a dog coming in from the rain and lost himself in the heat of his passion.

If anyone asked how he could even think about making love at this moment with all that awaited him on the job, he would have the answer. For the moment at least, it was the only thing that made him feel safe. Maybe that was the greatest reason of all to admit to love, to care for someone more than yourself. The loners weren't just lonely; they were afraid.

A smile, a touch, a kiss, whispers in the darkness, someone to hold you, all conspired to build a fortress around you. You cuddled beside someone who like you had confessed to herself that on this journey it was necessary to hold someone's hand and share dreams.

And of course, help you climb up and out of nightmares.

Four

He had slept in Central Park. When he lowered his head on the grassy knoll and closed his eyes, he wondered if he would awaken or die there. If he died, his body would be discovered and, because he had no identification, be relegated to the obscurity of the homeless and stuffed away in some unmarked plot. There would be no evidence of his renewed existence. Worst of all, they would go on unpunished. His revenge would be buried right beside him and he'd sleep with the frustration into eternity. That sort of punishment rivaled something mythological. It ached him just to think about such a possibility.

The warm sunlight on his face opened his eyes with glee. He sat up and looked around. He was still alive, but even more importantly, something unexpected was happening. He felt stronger. He was actually hungry, and he hadn't been hungry like this for some time. Beside his mother's money, he had robbed the taxicab driver and had more than six hundred dollars extra. He rose and made his way to a small coffee shop on Madison and 61st, seemingly growing more invigorated with each step he took. When he entered the shop, the aroma of coffee, bacon and eggs raised his expectations even further. He surprised himself with how much he ordered.

While his breakfast was being prepared, he went into the men's room and did the best he could to clean up. He could see that the short-order chef and the cashier were close to turning him away, thinking he was really just another homeless man who had scrounged up enough money to order some breakfast. He deliberately made his whole wad of bills obvious and that seemed enough to get him a ticket to remain.

In the bathroom he regretted not having a razor. The gray stubble had thickened over his cheeks and chin and made it look like he had sandpaper for skin. However, his lips had more color and some of the pallor in his complexion had diminished. His eyes looked clearer. Maybe it was his imagination or his hope, but his hair looked darker and thicker, too. When another customer entered the bathroom, he stopped studying himself and left quickly.

He returned to his seat and ate with a ravenous appetite, gulping three cups of coffee and finishing all the toast. He used a small piece to lick the plate clean as would a dog. He could feel eyes on him, imagining their comments and thoughts as he devoured his food, but he ignored it, left a hefty tip for spite, and walked out.

The rapidly warming day filled him with a joy he had no longer thought possible. For a moment he stood there with his face in the direct sunlight, smiling like some five-year-old. He even laughed aloud and then realizing his actions might attract attention, he quickly gathered himself and walked on.

As he made his way up Madison, he avoided looking at everyone who passed him going in the opposite direction. The expressions on the people who had seen and heard him laughing before made him nervous. The possibility that someone might look into his face and realize who and what he was frightened him. Nothing would be worse, would be more of a disappointment, than to be given the opportunity to get so close and then fail. That would be almost as much torture as what he had already endured.

When he had first started out on this mission, he was afraid his memory would disappoint him and he would follow one dead end after another, wasting what little time he had left. He was buoyed by how much he did remember and grew more confident with the resurrection of even more detail. He noticed that it really was getting easier for him to walk, too. His legs didn't wobble nearly as much as they had the day before, and the aches and pains he had experienced in his hips and lower back were practically non-existent. Do I dare hope? He wondered. After all, the image that was reflected back at him when he gazed into store windows was still unrecognizable.

When he reached the church, he hesitated. Despite his disgust with religion, he was not able to completely discount the presence of God in the world. Goodness knows, his mother had done all she could to impress upon him that even if he could get away with something wrong, he did not escape the eyes of God and he was depositing sins and blasphemies in an account that would be called up on Judgment Day. Although he was able to get past the threat, he never completely rid himself of the fear. The church was intimidating.

But the church was ruled and run by men, he told himself, and their motives were really no higher than his when they were stripped down to cold reality. There was the same thirst for power and the same selfish need to please yourself and build your own ego. They just did a better job of disguising it, and where corrupt politicians wrapped themselves in the flag, these men of the cloth wrapped themselves in pages of the Bible. They compromised to move up the ladder of wealth and power as much as anyone. He comforted himself and steeled his nerves by concluding that they were no better than he was.

He headed for the rectory, eager to see the look on Father Martin's face when the man confronted him. The priest had visited him at least a half dozen times in prison. He had evinced such confidence and projected the authority and the complete assurance that he had divine permission to approve all that had been proposed. After all, according to Father Martin, it was another weapon in the arsenal to defeat Satan or satanic forces at work in the world.

'You're redeeming yourself in the eyes of the Lord by volunteering for this, Bradley,' he told him. 'I know you haven't been a religious man and I know this has brought great pain to your mother, but I truly hope this will restore your faith, for it is a merciful God who has enabled man to find this solution, a solution in which you pay for your sins, but become restored faster so there will be time to build your good deeds, and win back the love of God. Bless you, my son.'

The priest's eyes were soft and angelic and his touch comforting. His voice was mesmerizing. He looked like he truly cared what happened to Bradley's soul, that Bradley's fate was intrinsically linked to his own. He gave him the sense that if Bradley turned him away, he would suffer just as much.

The fact that Bradley could recall this speech in such detail didn't really amaze him as much as the other things he was recalling. After all, Father Martin had truly had the most significant influence on him. He revisited those words often during his period of decision. The priest practically branded them with a molten hot cross into his brain.

How clever they were to include every angle, he thought: religion, science, law, politics. Each had its arguments and its justifications. Each had its promises and its rewards for him, and now each would know him and what they had done. He wouldn't just make them eat their words; he would make them eat their deaths.

He rang the buzzer on the rectory door and wiped his mouth with the back of his hand. Specks of egg yolk appeared on his brown spotted skin. He really had gone after that food like some wild animal, he thought and smiled at the impression he had made on the waitress and cook. The waitress had quite a full figure, albeit wide hips that looked like a rocket launching pad. He could launch something off her, he told himself and chuckled. Could he be mistaken? Did he have other appetites rejuvenating as well?

A short, fragile seeming man who looked like he was prematurely balding answered the door. He wore a white shirt opened at the collar and a pair of black pants. He had an unusually narrow nose and two beady black eyes. How could he breathe in enough air through those small, pinched nostrils? Bradley thought he resembled an insect. There was something at once feminine and childish in his smile, in the stretch of those thin, slightly orange lips and small teeth glittering like tiny precious stones in the sunlight.

'Good morning,' he said smiling as if Bradley had been coming here this time of day every day for years. 'How might I be of assistance?'

'You might be of assistance by telling Father Martin I am here to see him.'

'And who might I say is calling?' he asked. He sounded like he was attempting an Irish accent, but doing it badly.

'Bradley Preston Morris,' he declared with an exaggerated flair stimulated by this wisp of a human being taking great care with his diction. 'Himself,' he added. 'In the flesh, as they say.'

The young man blinked his long eyelashes rapidly and then suddenly hardened. His whole body was folding into a defensive posture like a caterpillar curling. His eyes seemed to freeze into glass orbs and his lips turned down in the corners.

He lifted his small shoulders as well, making it look like his neck lowered as would a submarine periscope when the captain urgently screamed, 'Dive, dive, dive!'

'Who did you say was calling on Father Martin?'

'Just tell him Bradley Morris,' Bradley replied with a directness and firmness that clearly stated an impatience for the slightest delay. Gentleness was over.

'Wait here,' the man replied sharply and closed the door in his face.

Bradley felt a swirl of rage building in his chest. He wasn't confident of the strength in his arms and he didn't know how long he could exert his muscles anyway, but he was filled with a burning desire to wrap his hands around the man's neck and squeeze the arrogant life out of him. The surge of anger, however, was followed with an all-to-familiar sense of utter exhaustion. Once again, he felt his body slipping off his bones and looked down to see if a puddle of his flesh was beginning to form at his feet.

The door was abruptly opened again and Father Martin stood there gaping at him. He looked like he was sniffing him as well.

'Bradley?' he asked, a look of incredulity molding itself in his face.

'Yes, Father, it is me to the bone, Bradley Morris.'

Father Martin simply stared and then he realized what he was doing and stepped back. 'Come in, man,' he said with sudden urgency, looking past him to be sure he wasn't followed or accompanied by anyone. 'You're alone?' he asked, not hiding his utter surprise underlined with a hint of panic.

'Yes, Father, as alone as ever,' he replied.

So, all this is still clandestine, Bradley thought as he stepped into the rectory. The world knew nothing after all. That was good. Knowledge was power and he had knowledge.

He gazed around the living room, surprised at how simple it was. There were only religious icons on the walls, a very dark gray rug on the floor between the sofa and two cushioned chairs, and an oval cherry wood table. There was nothing on the table.

'Please, have a seat,' Father Martin said. He turned to his assistant. 'Bring us some cold lemonade, please, Gerald.'

'Yes, Father,' Gerald replied, glancing suspiciously at Bradley as he left.

Bradley sat on the first cushioned chair and Father Martin lowered himself on to the sofa. He was a tall man, easily more than six feet one with broad shoulders. Bradley recalled him saying something about playing football at Notre Dame. His dark-brown hair was streaked with gray along the temples, but still quite full. He imagined him to be in his fifties.

Father Martin clasped his large hands together, the fingers moving like baby snakes over his knuckles.

'Aren't you going to ask me how I feel, Father?'

'I imagine you're about to tell me,' Father Martin said.

The soft, angelic smile and loving eyes were buried under a look of anticipation, suspicion and a bit of anger. The man was annoyed that he had simply shown up at his door like this without any warning. Was he mad at me, Bradley wondered, or more angry at his fellow conspirators for not giving him the heads up? Whatever, it wasn't very Christian of him to look and sound like this. Where was the mercy and compassion now? Where was all that holy talk? God's voice? The priest was recoiling like a snake moving into a protective stance. Thieves and scoundrels . . . all of us, Bradley thought.

'Betrayed, Father, I feel betrayed.'

'Why are you in these clothes? Where have you been since . . .?

'My death?'

Father Martin didn't respond.

'I heard I had a very nice funeral. You weren't there by any chance, were you, Father? I simply don't remember all that much about it.'

Before Father Martin could reply, Gerald entered with a tray carrying a pitcher of lemonade and two glasses with ice cubes in the glasses. He placed it on the table between them and then carefully poured a nearly equal amount in each glass.

'Anything else, Father?'

'No, Gerald, thank you,' Father Martin said, but Gerald didn't leave. 'That will be all, Gerald,' he added firmly and Gerald glanced at Bradley and then left.

Bradley lifted a glass to his lips and drank. He was incredibly thirsty. He emptied the glass without a breath and put it on the table. Father Martin looked at him as if he had just completed an amazing task, and then he sipped at his glass of lemonade.

'Yes, Bradley, where have you been since your death?' he asked. 'You're not working somewhere, are you?'

'Heavens no. I've been in a clinic or hospital, Father. Don't know what they call it exactly. I was on some rather restricted floor, if you get my drift. At the time it didn't matter. I wasn't having visitors. It was, as you might imagine, unexpected.'

'Unexpected?'

'Yes, Father. You see, I was brought there with the expectation I would soon die.'

'Die? But I was under the impression . . .'

'Oh, yes, tests were done on me before that and I thought everything was moving along as planned, but pretty soon, I sensed that things were moving along too fast, if you get my drift.' Bradley smiled. 'Someone forgot how to put on the brakes.'

'I don't understand,' Father Martin said. 'That's not what I was told would occur.'

'Funny, it's not what I was told would occur either. What do you think, Father? Will I be even more redeemed now, now that I have suffered more than I was sentenced to suffer? God should take that into consideration, don't you think?'

Father Martin shook his head. 'Why did this happen?' he asked, not visibly angry. 'You're not the first. I was told there was solid proof of success. I even met one and I know he hasn't turned out like you, so there has to be some explanation. When they transferred you to that clinic, they were surely looking for an explanation.'

'You mean they didn't just put me there to die? Well, that should make me feel lots better . . . an explanation. I wonder if they ever found one perhaps to help the next poor sucker.'

'I'll check into it. For now, however, I'd advise you return to the clinic. I'll make some calls and—'

'Oh no, Father. I can't return. I've lost my faith, you see.'

'You can't just wander about in this condition. Something should be done about this, Bradley.'

'Oh, something will be done, Father,' Bradley said. He poured himself some more lemonade and gulped it down. Then he wiped his lips with the back of his hand and flicked it to get the lemonade off as he stood up.

Father Martin sat there looking up at him. 'Where are you going to go, Bradley?'

'I was thinking of visiting with Mr Temple. I can see him now, standing there beside you, explaining all the legalities, the way I would continue with my life under a new identity, the job, the place to live . . . all of it. He even went through that charade of having me sign those papers, remember? The ones with his signature on? The corporate lawyer, very impressive. Even you were impressed with him and those documents, weren't you, Father? I haven't seen those papers since. Have you seen them? I wonder where they are?'

'Now, don't go off on some wild goose chase, Bradley. As I said, I'm going to make some calls and—'

'No, Father. You've done enough,' Bradley said. 'I didn't come here to ask you for any more help.'

Father Martin nodded. 'I understand your bitterness, my son.'

'Good, Father, because I don't.' He paused and looked at the wall behind Father Martin. 'There's Jesus on the cross wondering how the hell he ended up there, I'm sure. He and I have a lot in common, the only difference being I had encountered more Judases than he did,' Bradley said.

He walked around the sofa and touched the icon.

Father Martin turned to watch him and then looked away.

Bradley started around the sofa, paused, drew out the knife he had taken from his mother's set of steak knives and had used on the cabdriver, seized Father Martin's hair and pulled his head back just enough to expose his throat. He was pleasantly surprised at his speed and agility when he sliced through the priest's Adams apple.

The priest gagged, his head dropping forward when Bradley let go of his hair, and then he toppled slowly from the sofa to the floor, choking to death on his own blood.

'Bless me, Father,' Bradley said as he looked down at him, 'for I have sinned.'

He paused, took another long gulp of lemonade, wiped the glass clean of his prints with a napkin and then stepped out of the rectory.

The sunlight was stronger, the warmth greater. He smiled and, rejoicing in the bounce in his steps, hurried away to join the parade of people walking briskly down the sidewalk in the upscale East side neighborhood where the windows of shops were filled with the world's most expensive designer clothing, jewelry, shoes and cosmetics. It was a world of promise ready to deliver itself to the rich and famous.

He was neither, but he was none the less as pleased to be there as any of them were.

'What is all this?' Tucker asked Palmer. He was sifting through documents. Tucker looked at one. 'Bradley Preston Morris' death certificate? Why did you get all this stuff?'

'I didn't see any harm in checking into her story before we talked further with the mother. Something still bothers me. There has to be some connection, Tucker. Why would this guy go to rob Ceil Morris? Why her of all people?'

'Oh no. You're not still going to pull that intuition stuff on me with this, are you?'

Palmer didn't answer. He continued to carefully go through the documentation from the state prison system and the criminal records. He stared at the photographs of Bradley Morris for a few moments and then sat back in his chair.

'Maybe what we should do is get a computerized projection as to what this guy would look like in his nineties and bring it over to his mother to confirm the disguise used. That might help us locate this killer.'

'Really? You sure you don't think we should start with some of the people who signed these documents, especially this Dr Crowley who signed the death certificate?' Tucker asked, half-kidding. 'You know, demand to know why he said someone was dead when he wasn't?'

Palmer considered the document again. 'Woodbourne. That's about a two-hour drive,' he said. 'Maybe we should do just that.'

'I was just kidding, Palmer. We can't justify such a trip, especially with the story Mrs Morris gave us.'

Palmer was silent. Tucker raised his eyebrows.

'Palmer, are you listening to me?'

'Yes, I know, I know. All right. Let me give this picture to Wizner to show her when he goes to see her about the robbery. Maybe he can bring Mrs Morris down to work with an artist and help us get up a reasonable current likeness.'

'My guess is he's gotten rid of the disguise by now,' Tucker said. 'He was smart enough to wipe the taxicab handles; he's smart enough to change his appearance.'

'Still, it won't hurt to have both the actual likeness and his creative changes. Maybe we'll release them side by side. We've done that before with perps who tried to change their appearances.'

'Um. Yeah, maybe, but I don't trust you,' Tucker added. 'Next thing I know, you'll find out when this Morris character was born and bring out one of those astrological charts or something.'

Palmer laughed. 'Don't worry. Be right back,' he said rising.

Tucker sat down to read some of the documentation while Palmer went off to take care of the artistic rendition using Mrs Morris' information. He didn't look up when Palmer returned.

'Intriguing stuff, huh?'

Tucker smirked.

'C'mon, admit it. Didn't you see that the convict who attacked and supposedly killed Bradley Morris was killed himself in prison soon after?'

'So? All it means to me is we're apparently doing a very bad job of protecting rapists and killers in prisons.'

'You need a little dose of paranoia,' Palmer said. He started to put the documents in a large envelope just as the phone rang. Tucker took the call.

'Tucker, homicide,' he said and listened. As he did so, he lifted his gaze to Palmer. 'We're on our way,' he said and cradled the receiver slowly.

'What?'

'Our senior citizen just killed a priest uptown, Father Martin.'

'So, he didn't discard that disguise,' Palmer immediately said.

'Well OK, maybe it isn't a disguise,' Tucker relented.

'Was it a robbery?'

'I don't know. We'll see. There was no mention of a robbery, but why else would he kill a priest?'

'Something tells me we have a ways to go before any of this makes any sense, Tucker,' Palmer said. He nodded at the documents and then he and Tucker headed out.

There were four black and whites parked outside the rectory and two uniforms guarding the front entrance when they pulled up. Newspaper reporters were just arriving.

'Who's been inside at the scene?' Tucker asked immediately. The taller policeman confessed to entering.

'I had to look. Father Martin's clerk was quite hysterical,' he said, 'but I was really careful.'

'Where's this clerk?'

'He's inside, in the kitchen with Sergeant Lewis.'

Palmer and Tucker put on their gloves and shoe covers and entered the living room. Father Martin lay in a fetal position, the pool of blood spreading a stain on the rug beneath his neck. They heard crying coming from the kitchen and went in. Gerald was seated with his hands over his eyes, his body shaking with his sobs. Sergeant Lewis stood beside him, his right hand on Gerald's shoulder. He looked quite shaken himself.

'I knew Father Martin pretty well,' he immediately explained.

Gerald looked up slowly, wiping his cheeks with his handkerchief and taking a deep breath.

'This is Gerald Spenser, Father Martin's clerk,' Sergeant Lewis said.

'Did you witness this?' Tucker asked Gerald.

He slowly lowered his hands, sucked in his breath and shook his head. 'No, I brought them lemonade and then I left. I heard the man leave and looked in.' His face began to crumble again. 'Father Martin's body was still quivering. I never felt as helpless as when I saw the . . . ghastly slash in his throat and all that blood.'

'Did you ever see the man before?' Palmer asked.

Gerald shook his head.

'Anything missing?' Tucker asked.

'No,' Gerald said and then bitterly added, 'just Father Martin's precious and holy life.'

They heard the CSI team arriving. Tucker looked in on them, but Palmer remained with Gerald and Sergeant Lewis to continue gathering information.

'Was he dressed in coveralls?' Palmer asked.

'Yes.'

'Quite elderly?'

'Yes and . . . no.'

'Yes and no?'

'Well, he looked like my grandfather, but he had . . .'

'What?'

'More energy,' Gerald said and shrugged. 'I'm sorry. I know I'm not making any sense, but . . .'

'Had you ever seen him here before?'

'No.'

'Could he have been in a disguise, make-up?'

'Maybe, but if so, it was a damn good job,' Gerald said.

'What else do you know about him?'

'What else? All I know about him is his name,' Gerald said.

'How did you know that?'

'He gave me his name when I greeted him at the door. He seemed to want to be sure Father Martin knew it was him.'

'What name did he give you, exactly?'

'At first, he said Bradley Preston Morris. He was somewhat sarcastic. I should have realized he wasn't right. I should have known. I . . .'

'So Father Martin knew him, knew Bradley Preston Morris?'

Gerald looked up quickly. 'I didn't say that.'

'Why would the killer make a point of giving you his name if Father Martin didn't know him?' Palmer asked softly.

Sergeant Lewis looked at him and then at Gerald.

'I don't know everyone Father Martin knows,' Gerald said. 'He meets so many people. I mean, met,' he added sadly.

'What about this guy? Do you know something about him?' Sergeant Lewis asked Palmer.

'If it's the same guy, he apparently killed a taxi driver right near Lincoln Center last night. Same MO.'

'He gets around. Mr Spenser here told me the guy looked pretty old, "too old to be dangerous to anyone except himself" were your exact words, were they not, Mr Spenser?'

Gerald looked at Palmer and nodded. 'Well, I mean . . . there was no way for me to know what he would do. I thought he was just some homeless person Father Martin had taken some interest in helping. He was quite . . . disheveled. He smelled, too,' he added and wiped his cheeks with a handkerchief, dabbing them gently. 'But I should have paid more attention to my instincts. As I said, I felt he had this . . . underlying energy. Something didn't jive.'

'After you let him in . . .' Palmer thought a moment.

'After you let him in, did you hear any of their conversation?'

The way Gerald's eyes twitched convinced Palmer that the man had eavesdropped, but wouldn't admit it.

'Accidentally, of course,' Palmer added hopefully. 'I mean,

anything you heard could help us find this guy before he hurts someone else.'

Gerald shook his head emphatically. 'I don't know any more about him. I don't know anything else,' he said firmly beginning to sound petulant.

Tucker stepped back into the room. 'He wiped the glass of lemonade,' he announced in disappointment. He glanced at Gerald and then said, 'It looks like he took Father Martin from behind, the angle of the slice,' he added.

Gerald looked down quickly. Palmer sensed something. It was like a tiny buzzer going off inside him.

'You saw the murder, didn't you?' he asked Gerald.

'I . . .'

'You saw him kill Father Martin,' Palmer insisted.

'I didn't see him actually kill him. I . . .'

'What did you see, Mr Spenser? Your failure to be forthcoming could hamper us and leave this guy out there to do something else just as terrible.'

'I glanced through the door and saw him standing by the crucifixion sculpture, the one in brass. He stroked it and mumbled something. Then I thought when he turned, he might see me watching so I quickly walked away.'

'He touched the sculpture?' Tucker followed. 'You saw him do that?'

'Yes.'

'Maybe he left a print on it,' Tucker told Palmer and turned to talk to the CSI unit in the living room.

'What else did you forget to tell us, Mr Spenser?' Palmer asked.

'Nothing. Honest. That's it.' He took a deep breath. 'You can't blame me for being . . . confused. Just a few hours ago, he was vibrant and alive and we were talking about an idea for a sermon,' he muttered, now looking like someone alone, thinking aloud.

Tucker returned. 'They're working on it,' he said. 'Fingers crossed.'

Palmer nodded. 'Mr Spenser, this is important to us,' Palmer continued. 'Do you know of any business, any contact Father Martin might have had with inmates in prison or any of the prison authorities?'

'Business?'

'Why are you asking him that?' Tucker wanted to know. He had missed the beginning of the interrogation.

'He said the man identified himself as Bradley Preston Morris and told him to so inform Father Martin.'

'Is that so?' Tucker asked, his eyebrows rising.

'Mr Spenser . . . had Father Martin any contact with prison inmates?' Palmer asked again.

'Well, he was responsible for a program whereby members of the clergy from all faiths regularly visited with troubled souls.'

'Nothing else?'

'I don't know what you mean,' Gerald said. 'What other sort of contact?'

'No special interest in anyone in particular, possibly this man?'

'Everyone he comforted he gave special interest,' Gerald replied. 'I can't believe this has happened,' he suddenly added, looking at them all as if they were partly to blame. 'To kill a man like Father Martin and so gruesomely, too. He must be Satan himself. I need a drink of water. I'm feeling nauseous, dizzy. Maybe I can lay down a while?'

'OK. If you think of anything else, anything at all that might help us find this guy, please call me,' Palmer said handing him his card.

Gerald took it and nodded.

Tucker's cell rang. He stepped aside to take the call and then he nodded at Palmer, indicating they should go outside.

'We can't be more than a few hours behind this guy,' Palmer started to say and stopped. 'What now?'

'Mrs Morris.'

'What?'

'Wizner went to look for Mrs Morris at Folio's, but she didn't report to work and didn't call in so he went to her apartment . . .'

'And?'

'Found her keeled over at the front door of her apartment.'

'Not stabbed, too?'

'No. Looks like a heart attack.'

'And a convenient one at that,' Palmer said.

'Convenient for who?'

'Let's wait and see,' Palmer said. 'I get the feeling Gerald Spenser knows more about all this than he's telling us.'

'Why hold back?'

'Fear,' Palmer said.

'Fear?'

'You weren't in there with him when he was answering my questions. It was palpable,' Palmer said.

Tucker smirked. 'He also thought Bradley Morris might be Satan.'

'Maybe he is,' Palmer said. 'Maybe that's how he's come back from the dead.'

'You're kidding. I hope,' Tucker added.

'Yeah, I'm kidding, but,' he said looking back at the death scene in the rectory, 'you can't help but think it. Why else would he choose a priest as his next victim?'

'I agree. What happened to the good old-fashioned murders of passion and rage?' Tucker asked as they returned to their car.

'Maybe that's what this exactly is,' Palmer said.

'From your lips to God's ears,' Tucker replied.

They returned to the precinct. Later that day, Tucker reported the forensics on the statue.

'They lifted two great prints. They've been running them.'

'And?'

'Nothing. No hits. Even the computer is exhausted looking. It appears we have some senior citizen who just happened to start a criminal career late in life, someone without any previous record.'

'I don't think we can be so quick to assume so, Tucker.'

Palmer had that look on his face that Tucker knew all too well.

'Why not? What?' he asked. 'I know you're going to say something far out, Palmer.'

'I requested Bradley Morris' records. Guess what's missing.'

'Don't tell me this, Palmer. I'm warning you,' Tucker said and held his breath. Palmer nodded.

'His prints.'

'But he was in prison. He was convicted. You have his death certificate on the desk there. I read it. I read the report the warden submitted. There have to be fingerprints on file.'

Palmer stared at him.

'How do they lose his prints?'

'You tell me,' Palmer said rising. 'Or maybe you can wait until afterward.'

'Afterward? After what?'

'I think we need to take a ride, Tucker.' He looked at his watch. 'If we leave right now . . .'

'Where to?'

'To Woodbourne.'

'Woodbourne? You mean to speak to that doctor on the death certificate? What's his name?' He looked at the document. 'Crowley?'

'Yes. Let's start with him and go over to the prison and see if we can talk to the warden. If not there, at his home,' Palmer said.

Tucker shook his head, gazed at the documents and then looked toward the chief's office. 'You tell him any of this yet?'

'Not yet. It's just time and gas for now,' Palmer said.

'You're sure there aren't any prints on file?' Tucker asked again.

'If it wasn't for this death certificate and the report, I'd wonder if he even existed,' Palmer said. 'Not even a social security trail.'

Tucker nodded slowly. 'Man. You're lucky you're still unmarried, Palmer. You don't have to explain all this overtime to a woman who is too smart to be fooled by anything but the truth.'

'The truth's fooling us, too,' Palmer said.

Tucker didn't reply. He followed him out quietly instead. He had run out of arguments, and despite his reluctance to admit it, he was full of curiosity. Or what Palmer liked to call 'Good paranoia'.

Five

L ouis Williams saw the ambulance simply labeled EMER-GENCY VEHICLE pull into his driveway. Against his doctor's orders, he was having a cigarette. Despite the scientific evidence, the medical data and the people he had known who had died of either emphysema, lung cancer or heart failure, he could never accept that these coffin nails, as his grandfather referred to them, did all that much damage. They were valuable in prison and he held with others who rationalized away the danger by saying, 'Everything kills you. Don't eat this. Don't do that. Don't even breathe.'

He wasn't exactly brought up with, or associated with, people who were that intelligent anyway, he thought, as if that excused him from becoming an enforcer for a drug lord after a life of petty crime, a career move that sent him up the river for a ridiculous number of years. They might as well have given him life. He had been thirty-eight and sentenced to forty years with no hope of parole, and that was only for the crimes they could pin on him.

Until the warden called him into his office that day and introduced him to Dr Oakland, Father Martin, Mr Temple and some other guy who just sat there staring at him, he had little hope of doing anything but rotting away in prison. Even though he was quite capable of protecting himself and had the respect of most other inmates, he knew that the day would come when he would be a victim, whether he'd be raped or just beaten to an inch of his life. Every single day involved another battle or maneuver for survival.

And here were these distinguished looking, obviously powerful men offering him an opportunity to get out. They made it clear there were no guarantees, just very good possibilities and they justified their offer to him by telling him he would be doing something of great social value. As if that mattered to him. He could see, however, it apparently mattered to them. The priest in particular was very convincing, appealing to his fear of the unknown hell that awaited him. Father Martin had done his research, too, and knew Louis's paternal grandfather was an Anglican minister. Not that he ever had liked the son of a bitch. He was the one most apt to pull off his belt and give him a good strapping from time to time, all in the name of the Lord.

The offer to set him up with a new identity, a house and a job as a manager in a bowling alley was very enticing as well. He could have the day-time manager position or the nighttime, so he chose night-time manager. Who the hell wanted to get up early? Not that he really had to do anything. There was an assistant day manager and assistant night manager who did the real work. He would just strut about, sit at the bar, have a new life, a life he never even dared dream he'd have.

Of course, he would be absolutely prohibited from having the slightest contact with any of his former associates, but he long ago lost interest in them anyway, and they in him.

So why not do it? What were the alternatives?

They even permitted him to choose his new name and he decided he liked Brad Lords. It sounded like a movie star's name. Before he did anything else, he spent private time with an agent from the Witness Protection Program who schooled him on what his background was supposed to be. Although there would be no one out there looking to kill him, no one he had betrayed, he got the real sense that if he failed to follow the plan, their orders, and accidentally or deliberately revealed his true identity, they would have to eliminate him. Since they would have so much control of his new life, he had no doubt they could do whatever they wanted to him and get away with it. Who would know anything now? Who the hell would care? For that reason, he had the sense that they were a worse threat than anyone who he might have betrayed could be.

'If you can't do this, you'd better opt out now,' the agent told him. The man looked clean, sharply dressed, and more like a successful businessman, but he had eyes as cold as any killer Louis had ever met.

So he studied his new biography. He listened to their instructions and then when they thought he was ready, he was woken one night and escorted out of the cell to a waiting limousine. The men in the car with him were impressive, big, hard cut, no nonsense guys who were so confident of their ability to kill him in an instant, they didn't put any cuffs on him. He sat quietly, now not only interested in what would come, but a little afraid. What the hell had he agreed to do?

The ride was surprisingly short. He was escorted into a building and taken to what looked like a hospital room where he was told to undress and get into a hospital gown. No one really spoke to him except to give him orders. The nurse was at least kind enough to tell him her name, Miss Pearson. Another nurse came in after her, but she didn't introduce herself. He learned her name by listening to Miss Pearson call her Mrs Randolph. He thought it was peculiar the way they both addressed themselves as Miss and Mrs. It was as if they hadn't known each other or worked in this place very long and were certainly not friends at all. Maybe they weren't. What did any of that matter anyway?

He spent two weeks in that place even after Dr Oakland decided he was a success. After that he was kept in a housing facility and his reprogramming to become someone else just the way the agent from the Witness Protection Program had described continued. Finally, after numerous lab tests, examinations, X-rays, whatever, someone put the stamp of Good Housekeeping on his file and he was brought here and set up just the way they had promised.

He had no complaints.

He was going on eight months now, and he had even struck up a relationship with a waitress at the bowling alley restaurant, Alice Nicholas. She told everyone she was thirty-eight, but he checked her papers and found out she was almost forty-five. He didn't reveal it, however. After all, he was lying out of his teeth as well, wasn't he? In fact, except for his love of Italian food, he couldn't even remember a single thing he had told her that was true.

Lying had always come easy to him, even when he was an infant. He had a built-in fear and distrust of the truth. You always lied first, he thought, to be sure there were no land mines out there, and then, you gradually slipped in some truth when it was absolutely necessary – and only then.

Alice was divorced with no children which made it easier.

They were quickly becoming an item. She had moved some of her things into his house and spent four to five nights a week with him. Of course, he had dreamed of having younger women, but he was realistic now. He had some money, a good paying job, some respect, a modest home in a development, a decent car and, most of all, the best medical treatment and attention anyone could hope for, regardless of their wealth and position. It came with the territory.

All he had to do was lead a clean life and permit them to keep up his medical records and evaluations periodically, which was no burden. It occurred, or was supposed to occur, every three months. He had already experienced two evaluations. The only thing that was strange about that was he was made to wear a blindfold when he was taken back to the clinic. Obviously, he was not permitted to know where it was. They even examined him in a room without windows so he couldn't look out and see the surrounding area. And when it was time to go, he had to put on the blindfold and be lead out like a blind man.

Small discomforts for what he had now and where he would have been otherwise.

'What the hell are they doing here?' he muttered aloud as the two paramedics got out of the ambulance, went to the rear, and took out a gurney. They moved quickly toward his front door. He stepped back from his window abruptly and froze when he heard them ring the doorbell.

'What the hell's going on?' he shouted to no one in particular and went to the door. 'What is this?' he demanded before he had fully opened the door.

'Easy, Mr Lords,' one of the paramedics said pushing the door so he couldn't close it and stepping in. 'We need to transport you ASAP.'

'What? Transport me? Why? Where?'

'It's an emergency, obviously,' the other paramedic said pushing the gurney through the doorway. 'It's best for your cover if you're taken out of here like this. Please put out the cigarette and lie on the gurney. You aren't supposed to be smoking.'

'This is nuts. You're not here because I'm smoking, are you?'

They stared at him.

'Look, no one told me about this. How can it be an emergency? What emergency? I'm fine.'

'It just came up. Like he says, it's an emergency. It's better if you cooperate. It will go faster. Thank you,' the first paramedic added assuming Louis would just do what they asked.

'Thank you? What the fuck . . .'

He looked from one to the other. He had never seen either of them and neither looked like real paramedics. He was familiar enough with deception and deceptive people to see something threatening in their eyes.

'I don't like this. Nothing's been done without some preparation, some warning. No one pulls any surprises. How do I know who you guys are really, huh?'

He backed up.

'We have simple instructions, Mr Lords. There's nothing we can do about it. We all follow instructions and that's that,' the second paramedic said. 'You should know that. Please, don't make this harder than it has to be.'

'I don't just go with anyone,' Louis replied. 'I got a card with a number on it to call if I ever have a problem. That's what I'm going to do now,' he said, 'so you just sit tight and wait.'

He turned to go to the wall phone in the kitchen. When he got there, he pulled out his wallet and searched for the card. All it had was a telephone number on it, no names, nothing else. It would be the first time he had ever used it. His fingers were actually trembling and for him that was damn unusual.

They took my courage too, he thought and wondered just what he had sold beside his soul. He muttered the number to himself and then lifted the receiver.

The tiny stick he felt at the back of his neck was like an insect bite. He reached back to slap it, but he barely got his arm up before the room spun and he sank into one of the paramedic's arms.

Through a mist of consciousness, he felt himself being lowered on to the gurney and then strapped in. He saw nothing, but heard the wheels going over the floor and felt himself being carried along and then lifted up and into the ambulance. The doors were shut. He tried to speak, was sure he had, but heard himself say nothing aloud.

Then he drifted into deeper darkness and silence.

Since there was no siren, none of the neighbors even went to their windows, much less step out to look. It was a blue collar neighborhood anyway and most, if not all, had full-time employment and were still at work. Anyway, what would it mean if anyone witnessed what was happening? What could anyone do? Why would anyone care? Few even knew he was there.

The ambulance backed up and started away. Only when it turned a corner and headed for the highway, did the siren sound.

But Louis didn't hear it. He didn't comprehend anything again until he heard someone say, 'There's a remarkable change on his EKG and his blood pressure, too. Better call Mr Dover right away.'

He heard some shuffling and mumbling. He was truly like a blind man. He felt sure his eyes were open, but he saw only blackness.

'Help me!' he was sure he cried. 'I can't see.'

He waited.

No one even acknowledged his pleas.

It was worse than being back in a jail cell. He was imprisoned in his own body.

Simon stood by the specimen's bed and looked at the blood test. This time the immune suppressor was working like a charm. He handed the report back to Miss Pearson without comment and smiled at his patient, not because he really gave a damn about him, but because his body was performing as Simon hoped it would. Mr Dover wanted to put everything on hold, but Simon's interpretation of that was merely that the releases would be on hold. His work, of course, had to continue, and this one was looking very, very good.

He had limited knowledge of personal information about his specimens. He preferred it that way. If he began to think of them as anything other than experimental vehicles, he might hesitate or make mistakes, or worse yet, not work as hard for this one or that, he thought, because of some subconscious moral pressure. Science has no room for any subjectivity. One convict is just like any other. His job was to help convince them he was their best hope for any reprieve, and that was all he would do.

They might not thank me immediately, but in time, they will, he told himself. The whole civilized world will.

He checked the man's skin. It had lost significant elasticity. The age spots were popping up like bubbles in a pond, too. One unexpected result was a cataract. The man's blood pressure rose, but that was expected. Arteries were hardening; a natural effect of aging. Yesterday, he had complained about a tooth and today, it fell out.

He told him the dentist would be in to see him and would work on a bridge for him. No problem. Actually, there were no unexpected results. No one had warned the specimen, but that was par for the course as well. After all, if they knew all the nitty-gritty details about what might happen to them, they might back out, even with the promise of freedom.

He glanced at the activity report, the man's physical strength and endurance. Everything was degenerating as anticipated. This was perfect. I'm back on track, he thought. This time nothing will stop me.

For a moment it struck him as ironic that his success was directly related to the man's loss of physical stamina, poorer hearing and eyesight and slower reflexes. Every other doctor would be doing all he or she could to prevent all this. They lived under the burden of 'Do no harm'.

'When am I getting out of here?' his specimen asked him.

Simon permitted himself to use his name when he spoke to him. 'Chester, believe me. It won't be long now. I need to run a few more tests over the next few days to be sure you're about where you are supposed to be.' He patted his hand just the way a good GP might to give his patient some comfort.

'I don't like this. It ain't what I thought.'

'I don't see why not,' Simon replied. 'Maybe,' Simon said smiling, 'you're just like anyone else. You were deceiving yourself. All of you pick and choose what reality you want to face. It's human nature.'

'All of us? What are you? Aren't you human?'

Simon just smiled at him.

'Ah, what the hell? I'll show you. I'll show all of you. I'm going to live a cleaner life,' Chester Elliot declared. 'Healthier life. No smoking, exercise, the right foods and vitamins. You'll see. I'll peal back these years.'

'Maybe you will. Good luck to you, Chester. I certainly wouldn't stand in your way.'

Chester Elliot grunted. 'I gotta piss again,' he said. 'Seems I'm pissing every few hours. Why's that?'

'Your prostate gland is enlarged. Very common for older men. If you want, we can do a TUR before you leave. Probably should,' he added thinking aloud.

'What the hell's that?'

'Transurethral resection . . . we widen the passage so you can urinate easier and not build up so much in your bladder. Very simple plumbing job,' Simon said. 'And usually it doesn't affect sexual activity. I bet you're already thinking ahead to Viagra,' he added smiling.

'Yeah, sure. Maybe I'll have that then.'

'Fine. I'll make a note of it. Relax for now or go pee.'

Before he could call for Miss Pearson, she surprised him by coming to the doorway of Chester's room. 'Excuse me, Dr Oakland, but I have Dr Hoffman calling you from the ER.'

'Hoffman? He's not here today,' Simon said. Miss Pearson just stared at him. She hated to be contradicted or corrected. He didn't like her because she was too much like he was. 'He called you from our ER, you said?'

'Yes, Dr Oakland. It's what he told me. He said he needs to speak with you immediately. He said it was urgent, otherwise I wouldn't interrupt.'

Damn right you wouldn't, Simon thought.

'I gotta pee,' Chester said. 'Can I get up and go?'

'What? Oh, yes. Miss Pearson, would you be so kind as to help our patient to the bathroom.'

Miss Pearson moved instantly to help Chester Elliot out of bed and guided him along with his IV rack toward the bathroom.

'What the hell's going on?' Simon muttered as he clipped Chester Elliot's chart back to his bed and walked out quickly. He went to the telephone by the counter at the end of the short hallway.

'Larry, what are you doing here?' he asked immediately. 'You're off today. I thought you had those tickets to the theater. What . . .?'

'Mr Dover brought me in.'

'What? Why?'

'To examine Louis Williams.'

'Louis? But I didn't authorize any examination. He's not due for a check-up for another month.'

Larry Hoffman was silent too long.

'What is it? What's happened?'

'I don't know, Simon. Dover called me on my cellphone. I was on the way into the city and had to turn back. Lillian was fit to be tied, but what could I do? I asked him if you were here. I didn't see why you couldn't or shouldn't handle it, but he ignored my question and told me Williams would be here when I arrived. He told me to have him evaluated immediately and not to confer with you until I had spoken with him first after I had the results. He made that very clear, Simon. Sorry, but you know that if—'

'What results?' Simon demanded interrupting.

'There's a remarkable rejuvenation occurring. His pulse, his heartbeat, his skin, eyesight . . . you name it, there are significant improvements.'

Now Simon was the silent one for a long few seconds. Improvements, he thought and cringed as if he had said something utterly disgusting.

'And you reported this to Dover?'

'Not five minutes ago.'

'What did he say?'

'He said to let you know immediately and also to let you know he would be coming to see you first thing tomorrow morning. He estimated around ten.'

'I don't understand. Why didn't he ask me to do the evaluation? And why didn't he call me after he spoke with you?' Simon asked and almost immediately answered his own question to himself. He didn't trust I would give him the true results. The man trusts no one. He probably had his own mother followed until she was taken to a rest home and then had her room bugged. As far as having Hoffman call me, Simon thought, that's Dover's immature way of showing me he's angry with me.

'I'm sorry. I don't know any more than what I've told you, Simon. You know I normally keep you up on anything the moment I know it. I—'

'Yes, yes, I know. What are you doing with Louis Williams now? Did he give you any instructions?'

'Yes. We're keeping him here.'

'Keeping? How long?'

'For the rest of his life, I imagine. So, not long,' Larry Hoffman said. 'We're sending him upstairs.'

They called that floor ICU when they spoke to each other in front of the nurses, but each thought of it as the Final Stage floor.

Simon held the phone until he realized Miss Pearson had come out of Chester Elliot's room and was staring at him. Then he cradled the receiver quickly and hurried out the door to the safety of his office where he could gather his thoughts and plan what to do next.

'Well, here's a change for a change,' Mrs Littleton said when Louis Williams was wheeled into the room that had been occupied by Sutter.

She, Shirley Cole and Freda Rosen had just begun their shift. Laura Randolph, the nurse who worked directly with Dr Oakland and Miss Pearson on the floor below, had escorted Louis Williams and was giving instructions to Shirley at the desk. Mrs Littleton and Freda watched them from Williams' doorway. The attendant and Mrs Littleton then transferred Louis from the gurney to the bed. Even though he was sedated, the attendant told her to help him strap down Louis.

'Why does he have to be strapped in?' she asked.

Freda overheard her. 'Just do what you're told to do,' Freda snapped and widened her eyes.

'I'm only asking,' Mrs Littleton said defensively. She looked at the attendant who avoided her and worked quickly. The moment he finished, he walked out, still without making a comment.

'I swear, some of the people working here are actually mute,' Mrs Littleton said looking after him. She stood beside Freda and watched the attendant join Laura Randolph. He said something to her and she turned and looked back at them.

'You should take a lesson from them. I don't know why you can't keep your trap shut,' Freda told her, 'and stop asking questions.'

As soon as Laura Randolph and the attendant left, Shirley started down the corridor toward them.

'First one under the age of eighty,' Mrs Littleton quipped. 'What's his problem? We had to strap him in.'

'He's here for observation,' Shirley said. 'Just like the others.'

'Observation,' Mrs Littleton repeated to Freda. 'What do they say? Some observation. It's like watching paint dry.'

'Let's hook him up,' Shirley said without comment. She entered Williams' room and Freda followed. They worked quickly, efficiently and in minutes had connected him to the monitors.

'He had to be strapped in. He's either dangerous to himself, or to others, or both, I bet. What did they give him?' Mrs Littleton asked.

'Don't you have things to do?' Shirley asked her. 'The other two are still alive.'

'If you could call it that,' Mrs Littleton said. She looked at them a moment and then left.

'She's going to get us all into trouble,' Shirley told Freda. 'I'm worried she's talking to people on the outside.'

'Oh, she's harmless, just a busybody.'

'Nevertheless, I've taken some precautions for us.'

'Precautions? What do you mean?'

'I told Mrs Randolph about our concerns.'

'Oh boy. You're going to get her fired for sure.'

'Well, the attendant told Randolph she was asking too many questions about Brad Lords.'

'Too many? She asked one question.'

'Do you want to lose this money because of her or from defending her?' Shirley fired back.

Freda shook her head. 'Hey, I've warned her just as much as you have, if not more. She's nothing more to me than a nurse's aide. Worry not.' She turned to Louis Williams. 'What's his chart say? How old is he?'

'Fifty-two.'

Freda drew closer to Louis and looked at his neck. 'See this?' she asked. Shirley joined her. 'Looks like he had a tattoo removed. I've seen what a mess these can be.'

Shirley shrugged. 'That should be the least of his troubles.'

'Why?' Freda took the chart and read it. 'These numbers aren't terrible. He's got better blood pressure than I do.'

'Whatever,' Shirley said.

They both turned sharply when Simon entered the room. Without a word, he went to Louis Williams and pulled back his eyelids to look at his eyes. Then he pinched his skin and took his pulse.

'We have him on the monitors, Dr Oakland,' Shirley said.

'I want a report on him every hour on the hour,' he said. 'Just call the vitals down to me.'

'Very good, Doctor,' Shirley said.

'Is there anything special we should look for when he regains consciousness, Dr Oakland?' Freda asked him.

'Yes. If he regains consciousness,' he replied and started out.

'Excuse me, Dr Oakland?' Freda asked.

'Yes, yes? What is it?' he asked impatiently from the doorway.

'I don't understand. You said if he regains consciousness.'

'What's to understand? If he regains consciousness, let me know.'

He left. Shirley and Freda looked at each other, then looked at Louis Williams.

'The man's vitals are very good, but Dr Oakland made it sound as if he didn't expect him to regain consciousness. And yet, they must think he will. Otherwise, why strap him in then? Sounds confusing. What do you think?'

'I don't think when I'm here,' Shirley said. She nodded for emphasis and walked out of the room.

Freda hesitated and then hurried after her, her own heart thumping enough to have her wonder if she should hook herself to a monitor.

Six

Peter Crowley started his jog late that afternoon. He had just put on his sweatsuit and running shoes two hours earlier when the call came from the prison. If it was just another inmate, he was prepared to put it off until he had run, showered and dressed, but it was the warden who was complaining about heart palpitations and he couldn't neglect the warden. This gig was too good to lose just so he could keep to his jogging schedule.

At fifty-eight, Peter was in remarkable health. He was as proud of his blood pressure, stamina, muscle structure and weight as a sculptor would be of his latest creation. In his mind the human body could be sculptured. He prided himself on being one of those rare doctors who actually practiced what they preached. When he bawled out a patient for being too heavy or smoking or just being a lazy son of a bitch and not exercising enough, the patient took it from him without that 'look who's talking' expression on his face.

Once again a bachelor after a rather nasty divorce, Peter chose not to diagnose his marriage as a failure, certainly not a failure because of him, but rather as a relationship that had simply not had the fuel to carry itself any further. He and Vera had run out of love. He enjoyed applying the jogging imagery. So much of life was like a sporting event anyway. Vera couldn't keep up with him so he had to leave her behind. It was as simple as that.

First, she couldn't stand that he was in better shape than she was and that she looked older than he did, even though she was actually five years younger. She did all the right cosmetic things: forbidding the suggestion of gray in her hair; had a personal trainer weekly; and after a second face lift, bathed in miraculous skin creams, but there was just something about the way she aged. Like some creeping crud, it moved up through her legs and into her face, shading and darkening, wrinkling and leaving shadows that wouldn't be washed out by any surgery, laser or otherwise.

It was her personality, he thought. She was too dark to start with, always looking pessimistically at things and people, dripping with cynicism, jealous of everyone and anyone, even her own daughter, and especially her younger more jovial sister. If there was ever anyone who lived believing the grass was always greener somewhere else, it was Vera. There was no better living illustration of Shakespeare's Othello syndrome, jealousy eating away at someone, than his ex-wife, he thought.

He was happy he had a profession, a job that took him away from home as much as it had these past years, especially the last five. And, Vera had no idea how much money he really had. Thank goodness for those offshore accounts, especially recently. He smiled to himself about it, thinking about the next vacation in Europe, one he would take alone, or . . . maybe not. He was thinking seriously about that young nurse at the prison. She was a bit of a wallflower, but oh how ripe and ready. He fantasized showing her the world, opening up new experiences to her, establishing new feelings, all because of his guidance. He needed someone to worship him again.

He shot down the driveway, sucking in the remarkably warm air for September in the Catskills and slowly increased his pace. He loved the way he could rise out of his body when he ran. He could feel his legs, powerful and long, carrying him on the wind, but his mind could break free and he could think and dream and not even realize how far he had already gone. He took long, even strides, moving his arms in synchronization, holding his head perfectly. At six two, one hundred seventy, he was really a natural runner, a fucking human cheetah, for Christ's sake, and he had the trophies from college to prove it.

He never noticed the hills and he ran smoothly down the other side of them. Occasionally, someone would beep a horn at him or wave and he would just lift his right hand without even looking to see who it was. He wasn't very interested in his neighbors anyway. His closest ones were businessmen, boring and self-absorbed, and there were actually prison guards living on this road as well. He didn't want to socialize with anyone from work. He was a little embarrassed by it. He knew some thought he was looking after convicts because he couldn't make an attractive physician's income in the outside world, but little did they know how good this job turned out to be. No, there was to be no hesitation when Warden Watson called for him.

He and Vera had gone to dinner a few times at Watson's home and they had the warden over at least twice at theirs. Michael Watson was a real politician, smooth – greasy smooth, – careful about what he said to people who mattered and even diplomatic with those who wouldn't have any direct effect on his life and career. He was just fifty, with a paunch and a face like a boxer, his nose a little flat, his lips a little too thick, his chin chiseled with a small, thin scar along the jawbone, and his balding head on a thick neck that ran smoothly into big shoulders. He had been a wrestler in college, but had been neglecting his health and gained too much weight ever since. His paunch was deceptively hard and seemed to be expanding daily. He drank too much and smoked. Peter was always warning him so it didn't surprise him to hear he was having some sort of a health issue.

When he had arrived at the prison, he had discovered Michael sprawled on his sofa, a cold cloth on his forehead. He took his blood pressure and found it far too high. His pulse was strong but too fast and he didn't like the color in his face. He was sweating profusely.

'Did you take any medications today, Michael?'

'Medications? Medications? No, no, no. Nothing.'

'You better go in, Michael,' he told him.

'The hospital?'

'You need tests run. Something's cooking here and I don't want to miss anything.'

'Jesus, I have so much on my plate today and tomorrow. Jesus,' he said.

Peter didn't like the way his pupils were dilating. He was scratching himself, too. If he didn't know him, he'd think he was on drugs.

'Listen, Michael, you may not have any plate tomorrow if you don't take care of yourself today. When did you start feeling like this?'

'Not until this afternoon. I got up, stopped at Willy's for breakfast as usual on the way in and . . .'

'Eggs, bacon, bagels?'

'No, actually. This morning I had oatmeal.'

'Oatmeal? You?'

'Mark Lewis, that BCI investigator I know, was there and he had just had it and recommended it highly. He sat while I ate and we talked about some of the crimes he's been investigating. Then I came to work.'

'And you had your lunch as usual.'

'Yeah, yeah, yeah. You really think I need to go in?'

'Yes, Michael.'

'I'll think about it. Nothing to take for now?'

'Not without some testing, Michael. I could give you exactly what you don't need and cause even more problems. Are you going to listen to me and go in?'

'Oh, sure, sure.'

'Listen, Michael, we both know this would be a bad time to cash in your chips.' He winked. 'We've got lots of living to do and we're bankrolled to do it.'

'You're not talking about any of that, Peter, are you?'

'Of course not. Have someone drive you, Michael . . .' He paused. 'Do you want me to drive you?'

'No, no, no, I'll get there. Damn it.'

Peter left him hoping he'd be listened to. He'd better, he thought. He sure had the symptoms of someone in a drug overdose, but he dared not even ask, even though so many people were closet addicts, taking too much of this or that. Somehow they thought because a doctor prescribed it, it was always safe, even when abused.

At least I did what I should, Peter thought. I'm a good doctor, he told himself. I'm a good man and I'm a good father. I was as good a husband as I could have been for twenty-two years. I have no regrets.

He ran on. Another horn sounded. He raised his hand, but this one didn't just go by.

When the car hit him from behind, he was well off to the side of the road. The moment he fell, he thought, Hey, this isn't fair. I'm doing everything right. I'm over enough to the side of the road.

His body sailed and when he came down, he landed on his head and slapped his torso on the macadam. He was able to get out one groan and even start to turn before the wheel hit him in his ribs and the car rode over him, crushing him into the street, squeezing the life out of him.

He died thinking this is not fair. I have all this opportunity and all this new money. I'm just about to start a whole new life.

Palmer and Tucker drove into the hamlet of Woodbourne and turned down Church Street just as the paramedics were loading Peter Crowley's body into the ambulance. Four township policemen were assisting and directing traffic around the scene. Off to the sides of the road, people had gathered in clumps and were watching and speaking softly, as softly as they did when they attended funeral services in church. After all, the air of something as solemn as death had fallen over the neighborhood. Even dogs hovering close to their owners seemed subdued, curious and a bit timid. Their instincts told them something very frightening and threatening to life had just passed through here. The sorrow it left in its wake was as dense as a humid summer's day.

Palmer slowed down and lowered his window. To illustrate that he and Tucker were not just curiosity seekers, he showed the patrolman his detective's badge before asking what was happening.

'Hit-and-run,' the patrolman said.

'Ah . . . sorry to see it. Maybe you can help us. We're looking for Dr Peter Crowley's house.'

The patrolman literally recoiled and then leaned forward. 'You're looking for Dr Crowley?'

'Yes, why?'

'That's him being loaded into the ambulance. He was the victim. He jogs on this road and someone struck him and then ran over him.'

'Ran over him?' Tucker asked, leaning over Palmer. 'Ran over him?' he repeated to be sure he was hearing right.

'Yes, sir. He died on the spot. There are no skid marks. Whoever did it, didn't try to stop. A neighbor noticed his body when she pulled out of her garage and called on her cellphone, but it was too late to do anything for him.'

Palmer and Tucker looked at each other.

'Any ideas on the driver?' Palmer asked him.

'Not yet. No one saw it happen. These are normally pretty

quiet neighborhoods, safe to run in. Hell, most of the time, a dog could sleep in the center of the street and not be disturbed for hours.'

The ambulance doors were shut and the paramedics went to the cab and got in to start away.

'He was the prison physician,' the patrolman said watching. 'Just got divorced recently.'

'Really?' Tucker said. 'Divorced, you say?'

'Yeah. There's one child, a daughter who just recently got married herself. Lives in Monroe. Married an advertising executive.' He smiled after relating all this detail. 'Small-town life. Everyone knows everyone else's business.'

'What about his wife?'

'She moved down to Monroe, too. Lives near her daughter.'

'How long have they been divorced?' Palmer asked.

The ambulance started away and the small groups of people watching began to disperse.

'I think about four months. Something like that. My brother is a corrections officer at the prison and knew him better than I did. You better move on or pull over. Traffic's starting again, people coming home from work.'

'Thanks,' Palmer said and drove slowly forward.

'Even I, a non-believer in intuition and psychic vision admit this is a helluva coincidence,' Tucker said.

'Um. A little too helluva. Let's get up to the prison and see if we can talk to the warden. His signature is on these documents.' He shuffled some papers. 'Name's Michael Watson. He was warden when Bradley Morris supposedly was killed and when the man who killed him was killed.'

'I have to also admit that it's one thing to accidentally hit a jogger, but to run him over as well? What the hell's going on here?' Tucker muttered as they headed for the prison.

'That's what we're trying to find out,' Palmer said smiling.

For the remainder of the ride, they were both deadly silent, but when they reached the prison and found out that Michael Watson was in the hospital with an apparent heart attack, their silence went so deep, it reached depths visited only by mutes. They got directions to the hospital and drove as quickly as they could, neither knowing what they expected to discover when they arrived.

What they discovered when they entered the hospital and

asked after him was that Michael Watson had expired. They stood there in the lobby looking at each other, both feeling as if they had experienced a combination of punches in the face.

'Bradley Morris' criminal records are non-existent except for his death and the surrounding events at the prison; there are no fingerprints on file; his mother, who claims to have seen him, drops dead before we can follow up; Father Martin, a priest who apparently knew Morris and ran a clergy visitation program at prisons was murdered by a man who fits the description of the man Mrs Morris claims is her son; Dr Crowley was just killed in a hit-and-run and the warden gets a fatal heart attack,' Palmer summed up. 'I feel like I'm in one of those houses on the side of a mountain with the earth below quickly sliding away.'

'Can we see the doctor who was treating Watson, please?' Tucker asked the nurse in the ER. She told them to wait. Nearly twenty minutes later, the ER doctor approached them. His name was Friedman and he looked no more than thirty years old at most.

'How can I help you, gentlemen?'

Palmer showed him his identification. He nodded. The nurses had apparently already told him there were New York City detectives waiting to see him.

'You're interested in Michael Watson?'

'Yes. Was this a straightforward heart attack?' Tucker asked. 'Straightforward?'

'What my partner means is, did Mr Watson have any history of medical problems? Was there any reason to suspect or expect such an event?'

'I'm not his personal physician so I am unaware of any chronic health issues, however I can tell you that we're fairly confident that this was a serious meth overdose.'

'What?' Both Tucker and Palmer said.

'We are contacting the local police about it, of course. His wife is here. She was taken completely by surprise, apparently. We haven't said anything to her just yet. We'll do a toxicology in the autopsy and have it all confirmed.'

'Meth?' Palmer asked incredulously. 'He was the warden in the prison.'

'I can't comment on anything. I can tell you that he came in on his own steam, in fact. He walked into the ER. He was very hyper, confused, babbling incessantly . . . classic symptoms. I managed to learn that his doctor at the prison recommended he be examined earlier. My guess is he was already showing symptoms that could suggest heart issues. He didn't come here right away, apparently. He said he started to feel even worse and finally thought it was best he come directly to the ER. We were setting him up for an EKG when he went into massive heart failure.'

'His doctor at the prison? Today?' Palmer asked.

'Yes, I believe he said today.'

'Are you aware of the fact that the prison doctor, Dr Crowley, was just killed? Hit-and-run?' Tucker asked.

Dr Friedman shook his head. 'I hadn't heard. How horrible.'

'OK, we'd like to see the autopsy report when it's completed,' Palmer said and gave Dr Friedman his card.

'I'll give you a call. Isn't it unusual for the New York City police department to be up here?' he asked.

'We're on a case that started there and has some tracks up here,' Palmer explained.

Friedman nodded.

'Thank you,' Tucker said. 'Meth overdose? This is weird. You'd think if he were a user, that he would have shown signs earlier.' Tucker said as they left the hospital. 'Of course, his wife could be covering up, pretending surprise.'

'A warden on drugs?'

'It's weird.'

'Let's go back and speak with Gerald Spenser,' Palmer said. 'I want to see if we can learn any more as to what a New York City priest had to do with an inmate in an upstate New York prison and maybe what he had to do with Warden Watson. I wasn't happy with his answers and reactions. He knows something he was reluctant to tell us.'

'That intuition thing again?'

'When in doubt, whip it out,' Palmer said.

They didn't get back into the city until nearly nine, having stopped on the way for a quick burger. They thought it was still early enough to pay Gerald a visit at the rectory and headed directly to it. There was only a dim light on inside so they suspected he wasn't there, but after they rang the door-bell, lights went on quickly and moments later, Gerald appeared, dressed in a blue robe and black slippers.

'Did you catch him?' was his immediate question.

'Not yet, Mr Spenser,' Palmer said, 'but we have a few more questions and hope you can help us with some information.'

'What?' he asked not making any indication that he was going to let them in.

'When I asked .you earlier if Father Martin was heavily involved with prison inmates, you said he was . . . I think you said something about troubled souls . . .'

'Yes, yes,' Gerald replied, visibly impatient. 'He was a leader in a program for convicts. I told you.'

'Did it specifically take him to a maximum security facility in upstate New York, Woodbourne, New York, to be precise?'

'Among others, I believe, yes.'

'How often?'

'I'd have to check his calendar to answer that.'

'What about the warden there, Mr Watson? Did they know each other well?'

'I don't recall him mentioning the warden before he went up there to visit inmates, so I can't tell you how well he knew him, or even if he knew him before the visits.'

'Any recent messages from Warden Watson for Father Martin?'

'No. I don't recall any message from any Warden Watson.'

'It's not just any Warden Watson,' Tucker said dryly. 'It's the warden of the maximum security prison in Woodbourne.'

'I have no recollection of messages,' Gerald said, the corners of his mouth dripping into his chin.

'What about these so-called troubled souls then? Did you keep track of the ones with whom he met?' Palmer asked sharply.

'It wasn't exactly the same as a doctor and his patients, Detective. We didn't keep records like that.'

'So you still don't recall him ever mentioning this man Bradley Morris, or him writing anything about him?'

'No,' he said quickly. 'I told you that the first time.'

'If you didn't keep records like a doctor, how can you be so certain so fast?' Tucker asked.

'I'm trying to be as helpful as I can,' Gerald replied. 'I didn't recall that name when you asked before and I don't now. Except of course . . . because of . . .'

'I'm still puzzled as to why Father Martin agreed to meet with him so readily,' Palmer said.

'I've already explained that Father Martin was that sort of priest, compassionate and accessible. It's not a big mystery.'

'On the contrary,' Palmer said. 'It is rapidly becoming a bigger and bigger mystery. If you know something more and are hesitating . . .'

'Why would I do such a thing?' He blew out some air and shook his head. 'Look, I'm still quite upset. We were together a long time. It's like losing a close member of your family.'

'What are you going to do now?' Tucker asked.

'What do you mean?'

'You lost your employer, your job, I imagine,' he replied.

'I've been offered something else,' Gerald said. 'I'm leaving next week for Pittsburgh.'

'So quickly? How could you be offered something so quickly?' Tucker asked as if he was angry about it.

'Father Martin left a very high recommendation in case I ever needed it,' he said calmly.

'How clairvoyant he must have been,' Palmer said.

'No. Simply considerate and caring. Rare these days, I know,' Gerald said. 'But we always hope a man like that will influence others. Is there anything else? I was just going to bed. I've actually taken a sleeping pill.'

'As soon as you get up in the morning, check his calendar. I'll call you to find out precisely how often he visited the prison in Woodbourne,' Palmer said sharply.

'Why don't you just check with the prison?' Gerald suggested. 'Call this warden directly. I'm sure they have records of whomever visits, especially maximum security. They're sure to be even more accurate.'

'Warden Watson is dead,' Tucker said. 'He died today.'

'Dead?'

His reaction was dramatic.

'Are you sure you don't recall him leaving messages for Father Martin, perhaps yesterday, today?'

'What? No. How did he die?'

'Why are you concerned if you don't recall him at all?' Tucker asked.

'He was another human being, Detective Browning. We should all be concerned about our fellow man. No man is an island.'

'Yeah, we'll see who is and isn't an island,' Palmer said. 'Check your books. I want to know what information you have. I'll be calling you in the morning,' he emphasized.

'And let us run the investigation,' Tucker added dryly. 'You leave your next address with us as well. You're a major witness in this murder case.'

'Oh, absolutely. I knew to do that,' Gerald said and then backed up and closed the door.

They stood looking at the closed door a moment before turning away.

'A regular cunt of a guy,' Tucker said. 'Makes my skin crawl actually.'

'Something is rotten in the state of New York,' Palmer said.

'Shakespeare returns in the nick of time,' Tucker quipped.

Seven

It was as if killing Father Martin hastened his rejuvenation. In fact, he seriously considered the possibility that as he delivered justice, he was rewarded with servings of youth. Of course, in his case his appetite for it was ravenous. All of his appetites were. Not only was he hungry again, but he was moving even faster, and when he paused at a men's store front window and studied his reflection in the glass, he thought he indeed looked younger. Invigorated and encouraged, he entered the store.

The salesman behind the counter looked up in shock. Bradley could read his thoughts. *What the hell does this hobo want in here where a pair of socks is probably more money than he has all week?*

'I need a full set of clothes,' he said. 'A pair of pants, a shirt and a jacket and tie, as well as socks and underwear. Keep it under $1500,' he added and put the money on the counter.

The salesman looked at the bills and then at Bradley. Without saying a word, he glanced at his racks. Bradley could hear the cash till adding up in the man's head.

'I think we can fix you up very nicely,' he said. 'Right this way, Mr . . .?'

'Morris. I'm Bradley Morris,' he said pointedly. He said it as if he expected the salesman to recognize his name. For a moment the man wondered if he should and then he smiled, nodded and went to the racks. After all, wasn't it a well-known legend that Howard Hughes lived like a hobo?

A little over an hour later, Bradley emerged. He needed a haircut and a shave, of course, but other than that, he cut a pretty handsome figure, he thought. He was standing straighter. His shoulders looked firmer and his stomach felt firmer as well. He still had hundreds of dollars, thanks to the bundle he took off the taxicab driver, so he walked briskly looking for a men's hair salon. He found one that advertised serving walk-ins and entered. Never before had a haircut and a shave helped him feel as good as this one did. The wrinkles he had anticipated under his facial hair weren't half as bad as expected. He sucked in the aroma of the aftershave, left his stylist a nice tip, and headed uptown. He knew exactly where he was going next.

On his way he stopped to have some lunch. He thought he would just have a burger, but he ordered a salad, French fries and a chunk of the better-than-sex chocolate cake for dessert. All he could think of was that some divine power was inserting itself into his life. What he had done in the past, his own sins, were obviously nowhere as large in the eyes of the Deity as what they had done to him. He was being restored to continue the pursuit of justice and the distribution of punishment. He beamed as he walked and then, when he saw a young, attractive woman in a green skirt and jacket smile at him, he felt his sexual urges come rushing back into him like an incoming tide. He was so happy he thought he might scream.

This tide brought with it another idea. He could go back to see his mother. She wouldn't be afraid now and he would promise her to return her money and more. Why not? He owed her so much. Funny, he thought, how he had never felt this remorse as strongly as he did now. Was that another consequence of his renewal?

I'm going to be a better person, he concluded. I'm going to be a good guy after I do what I have to do.

It brought laughter to his lips. People passing by looked at him and smiled. He wasn't threatening to them. They didn't see him as ugly or dangerous now that he was clean and in these expensive clothes. They were amused by his glee. This was wonderful; this was a whole new identity, truly a new life, the new life that they had promised. The restoration brought promise, hope, optimism and confidence. He knew just how he was going to finance this new beginning, too. He knew just how he would milk them. Again, this wasn't evil. They owed him. It was not extortion; it was justice.

Yes, he thought, it would be great to surprise his mother this time. He knew where she worked. He couldn't wait to see the look on her face.

Onward, he told himself and hailed a taxi.

He got out in front of Folio's and gave the cab driver a very good tip.

Makes up for my last taxi ride, he thought, and laughed. He wasn't sure which department his mother worked in or what floor, so he went to the information counter to his right. The young woman behind the counter was typing on a computer keyboard. He could tell from the expression on her face that it had nothing to do with her work. She didn't look his way so he grunted and she nearly leaped out of her seat.

'Oh, sorry. How can I help you?'

'I'm looking for a saleslady. Her name's Ceil Morris.'

Without responding, she looked at a directory and then said, 'Ladies lingerie, third floor.'

'Hey, thanks,' he said and flipped her what he was convinced was a winning smile. It simply brought a look of surprise to her bloated face.

He got into the elevator and then stepped out on the third floor. For a few moments, he stood there gazing about, hoping to spot her and sneak up on her. When he didn't see her, he moved quickly to another woman serving a customer.

'I'm looking for Mrs Morris,' he said interrupting. 'She works here.'

The saleslady looked up at him. 'Ceil? Oh. She didn't report to work today.'

'Didn't report?'

'Yes.'

'Why not?'

'I don't know, sir. Please excuse me. I'm with a customer,' she said.

He stood there glaring at the two of them and then turned around and headed for the elevator.

It was his fault, he thought. She was so disturbed by the events yesterday, she was sick, especially if she had discovered what he had taken.

He hailed another cab and nervously sat while the driver battled traffic.

'Don't you know any shortcuts?' he demanded when they were locked in a jam of trucks and cars. Just like the younger man he used to be, he had no tolerance nor any patience for delay or disappointment.

The driver glanced at him as if he had asked a very stupid question and shook his head.

'Fuck this, then,' Bradley said and got out without paying his tab.

'Hey!' the driver cried.

Bradley kept walking.

'Hey, you son of a bitch!'

He ignored him and quickly lost himself in a group of pedestrians crossing a street. He vaguely realized he would have to walk almost twenty blocks, but he didn't hesitate or even think about the subway. He just kept walking, a ball of rage twirling about in his stomach.

It took him the better part of an hour because of the crowds and traffic, but when he turned the corner and headed toward his mother's brownstone, he didn't even think of the distance he had covered nor the fact that he had been able to do it. Less than two days ago, he was dying in some hospital room. He charged up the short steps and went to the directory, found his mother's name and pressed the accompanying button. He waited and then pressed it again, waited and pressed it one more time.

Maybe she's out, he thought. Maybe she's just decided she doesn't want to go to work. Or maybe she's so sick, she's in bed and can't get to the buzzer. He looked up and down the street and considered what he should do next when he realized the outside door was not quite shut. It was the same way it had been when he'd first confronted his mother.

He pried it open as he had done before and stood in the alcove. Moments later, the inner door opened and he faced an elderly lady with curly gray hair and glasses as thick as goggles. The sight of him right in front of her caused her to gasp and step back.

'Sorry,' he said and entered. Without looking back, he went to the elevator and pressed the button for floor three. When it opened, he went down to his mother's apartment and pressed the buzzer on that door. Then he knocked. He waited, pressed the buzzer and knocked harder. If he hadn't been told she was sick and unable to come to work, he might have left, but he kept thinking of her inside, in her bed, maybe in trouble. He thought about it a little longer and then stepped back and turned his shoulder to hit the door hard. The frustration and rage wouldn't subside. He hit the door again and heard the wood frame crack. Then he stepped farther back and kicked it at the lock. The door flew open.

He stood there gasping, exhausted, but ecstatic at his jolt of energy and strength.

'Mom!' he called as he entered. He closed the door as best he could now with the lock shattered, and went directly to her bedroom.

The bed was empty, but made.

'Mom!'

It wasn't much of an apartment. In moments he had covered the bathroom, kitchen and living room. She wasn't there. He looked at the sofa upon which he had collapsed when he first came and then he sat and stared at the wall. If she didn't go to work, where did she go? Probably to the doctor, he thought and nodded. Yeah, the doctor. He'd wait.

He closed his eyes for a moment and when he opened them again, he realized he had fallen asleep. He wasn't sure how long he had slept, but it was obvious she hadn't returned. Frustrated and impatient, he rose and paced around the room, when he suddenly noticed a business card on the table by the sofa.

He picked it up and read it.

It was a card from a police detective, a Palmer Dorian. There was another number on the back, too. Why was there a police detective's card on the table? he wondered and then thought his mother had gone to the police or called them after she had realized he had robbed her.

My own mother was turning me in, he thought. She doesn't understand. I'm not the bad guy here. Why didn't she feel sorry for me, forgive me? How could she turn me in?

He shoved the card into his pocket. Under the circumstances, he didn't want to be here when she returned after all. When he stepped out of the apartment, the elevator doors opened and that same elderly lady whom he had confronted about an hour and a half ago stepped out.

She paused in obvious fear when she saw him and saw the opened door of his mother's apartment, the lock shattered and the door battered. He saw where her gaze had gone.

'Don't worry about it. I was worried about my mother,' he said. 'Do you know Ceil Morris?'

'Mrs Morris? Oh,' she said putting her hand to the base of her throat. 'Yes. Poor lady.'

'What do you mean "poor lady"?'

'She died. They found her dead this morning. Probably heart failure.'

He stared at her and shook his head. 'Ceil Morris died?'

'Yes, I'm afraid so. Who did you say you were?' she asked, incredulous, the words now sinking in.

'No one,' he said. 'No one.' He headed for the elevator.

'I thought you said you were her son. I didn't know she had a son. Oh dear.'

He looked past her as if he expected his mother to step out of the apartment to confirm that he was indeed her son.

'No,' he repeated and stepped into the elevator.

She stood there staring at him.

'It's not my fault,' he screamed at her and punched the button for the lobby. 'It's not my fault,' he muttered. 'It's theirs. Theirs!'

The doors closed.

When he stepped out of the building, he was still muttering to himself. As he headed up the street, he waved his fists at imaginary enemies.

Some nearby pedestrians widened the distance between them and him. It was one thing to laugh aloud, but to curse and shake his fist in the air was quite different. He glared at them and then he checked his actions quickly and hurried on before it was too late.

Palmer didn't realize how tired he was until he inserted his key in his apartment door. He closed his eyes for a moment and then he opened the door and entered, surprised to see the lights on and hear music.

Tracy appeared in the kitchen doorway.

'Where were you?' she asked.

'On a case. It took Tucker and me upstate. It's a nice surprise finding you here. What's going on?'

'Howard was so excited about a move I made two days ago with the shopping mall project in Westchester, he gave me a bonus and sent me home early. I had this nutty idea I would make this dinner for us to celebrate. It was a big bonus,' she added.

'Oh, I'm sorry.'

'It's not your fault. It's mine for assuming you would be around after work.'

'There is often no after work in my business,' he told her, 'and unfortunately, no bonuses or time off for good behavior.' He looked toward the dining room. 'What did you prepare?'

'Your favorite. Chicken Kiev.'

'Damn.'

'We can have it tomorrow night,' she said. 'You ate something, I take it.'

'Fast food on the way back.'

'Well, we can have a drink and relax together at least. I'll draw you a warm bath. You look like you need it and, if it's the case we're sharing, I'll want to hear.'

'Sharing?'

She kissed the tip of his nose and then his lips. 'You know of what I speak,' she said. 'Go get ready for your bath. I'll wash your neck and your back and whatever if you're nice and cooperative.'

'Sounds like blackmail,' he said.

She shrugged. 'Arrest me.'

'I just might put you in handcuffs, yes.'

'Ooooh. Don't get me too excited. I'll get the water too hot.'

He laughed and then headed for the bedroom.

'Oh,' she added before he got there. 'I see you have a message on your answering machine.'

'Do I? Thanks.'

He went to it and replayed the message. It was from Detective Wizner.

'Hey, tried to reach you earlier on your cellphone and then thought I'd leave a message for you here. I don't know if it's anything, but we got a call concerning that Morris woman. Seems her neighbor confronted a man who had just broken into Mrs Morris' apartment. He doesn't fit your perp's description, but she swears he told her he was Mrs Morris' son and then tried to deny he said it. Anyway, for what it's worth, there it is,' Wizner said. 'I'm going over to check out the place and speak to the neighbor. Her name's Lomar, Dorothy Lomar. Speak to you later if I come up with anything for you.'

'What was that about?' Tracy asked from the bathroom doorway.

'Not sure.'

'Why would someone else be robbing her home? She must have something very valuable hidden away. Maybe she doesn't even know it. It reminds me of that Audrey Hepburn movie, remember?'

'Whoa, Tracy. Slow down that runaway imagination. We're not in the movies here.'

'Just thought I'd help. Four eyes see more than two, my mother used to say. Or was it my grandmother?'

He laughed and returned to his bedroom. As he undressed to put on his robe, he thought about the irony that he was about to soak in a warm bath and enjoy happiness and pleasure while less than a hundred miles away, two families, relatives of both Peter Crowley and Michael Watson would be soaking in cold, dark sorrow. Often during some quiet moment, he would think about the statistical fact that every day, forty-five people were murdered in the United States. There were forty-five families in mourning right at this moment and forty-five new homicide cases opening, most nowhere nearly as complicated as this one involving that poor cab driver and Father Martin. Still, a number of people all over the country had lost someone they loved.

The public was so desensitized by the constant media reportage that one murder or violent death seemed like another and after a few seconds of seeing how the death had impacted on loved ones, it disappeared, popped like a bubble and was forgotten. For him and so many of his fellow law enforcement comrades, the judicial system and its handling of the offenders was more like a sewer system that had gone awry, plugged up and with leaks everywhere.

After some of the things he had witnessed even in his short career so far, it wasn't all that surprising to come upon a case where a convict was out there recommitting capital crimes, even one who had supposedly died and been buried. Surely there was some sensible explanation for all this. Somehow, somewhere, the system had fucked up again, he thought. In the end it will probably result in their discovering bureaucratic screw ups. People will acknowledge them, but few if any will bear any real responsibility. It will go on and happen again sometime.

Maybe Tucker was right to rely on the procedures, plodding through the steps and not dreaming of doing much more than following through, closing a case and then moving on according to the dictates of the system. Being too ambitious led to frustration and cynicism, which eventually made you darker and simply another part of the whole damn mess. He was too young to have these depressing thoughts. He wanted to find a way to fight them off.

'Why are you just sitting there like that, Palmer?' Tracy asked him.

He looked up, surprised to find himself sitting on his bed thinking.

'Just tired, I guess.'

She narrowed her eyes. 'You know I have a built-in bullshit detector,' she warned.

'You're in deep thought about this case. You are resisting relaxation. Either put it out of mind or share.'

He laughed. 'OK. It's probably better for me to talk to someone who will listen anyway,' he agreed. He rose. 'To the tub.'

She followed him into the bathroom. He felt the water, nodded, smiled at the bath oil she had added which already had bubbled up, and then dropped his robe. He lowered himself in the water and closed his eyes. For a moment he thought he might just fall asleep. The he heard her movements and opened his eyes to see her undressing and getting into the tub as well.

'Move down a bit,' she ordered, slipping in behind him. 'So I can do your back first.'

He did and she began.

'I'm in heaven,' he said. 'I don't even remember dying.'

'This is called living, stupid,' she said. 'No one bathes in heaven because no one can get dirty in heaven. It would not be heaven.'

'Um. You have a good point.'

'OK, start talking,' she said. 'And if there are ugly details, do not skip them.'

He reviewed the case with her while she gingerly moved the washcloth over his neck and around his back.

'It might very well be just a few coincidences,' she said.

'Yeah, Tucker's of that opinion, although he does admit

that something's out of the ordinary, someone's out there covering up something, if only a procedural error.'

'Have you found a way to explain Mrs Morris' description of this guy and then Father Martin's clerk's matching description in light of the fact that he was capable of committing two violent murders. Mrs Morris thought he was minutes if not seconds from being dead himself, right?'

'Well, I guess I have to go with the theory that whoever he is, he is in a disguise of sorts. Actually, taking on the appearance of an elderly man is clever.'

'So, someone skilled in make-up is an accomplice?'

'I don't know what else to think.'

'Maybe this guy was a make-up artist before he became a criminal. I'm sure there's a logical explanation.'

'Um.'

They were both silent, both their imaginations casting about for some explanation when they heard the phone.

'Shit,' he said.

'Just let it ring, Palmer. You've got an answering machine.'

'It might be Detective Wizner.'

They listened after the beep.

It helped that his caller was literally shouting into the phone.

'Detective Dorian, I am not responsible for my mother's death. I know who is and I'll take care of it. She shouldn't have called you in the first place. You stay out of my way and justice will be done.'

They heard him hang up.

Neither spoke. They both froze for a moment in the water, Tracy's hand on his shoulder.

'"My mother's death"?' she repeated.

Palmer rose out of the water and reached for a bath towel.

'He didn't sound old, did he, Palmer?'

'I don't know how old people sound anymore,' Palmer replied stepping out of the tub. 'I'd better give Tucker a call, play the message for him and tell him about Wizner's message.'

'How did he get your home number?' Tracy asked, still seated in the water.

Palmer paused. 'Yeah. I gave it to his mother.'

'She gave it to him?'

'No. He was gone by then, but Wizner said the neighbor saw someone who broke into the apartment. He must have found the card,' Palmer said. 'Or maybe . . . he's called from there just now. Maybe he's only just now found the card. We'll have to get over there.'

'You just got home. Didn't that Detective Wizner say he was going over there. He must have checked it out?'

'Maybe.'

He got out of the tub, grabbed a towel and started for the phone in the living room.

'Palmer . . .?'

'Hey, it's our case, Tracy. We have to follow through. Besides, even if he's gone, I want to be sure no one messes up any possible evidence,' he replied. He called the precinct first to see if Wizner had been to the apartment and back. He caught him just leaving.

He listened to the description Mrs Lomar had given.

'She didn't say he looked aged, then?'

'Older, but not aged, and very well dressed. She said he became quite agitated. You should see the job he did on the door. Tore out the frame, so I wouldn't call him exactly decrepit.'

'You guys lift any prints?'

'Yeah, we have plenty. I'm ahead of you there.'

'What?'

'We've got prints matching the ones lifted at Father Martin's. Same guy.'

'Same guy, but not in coveralls and very old looking?'

'You can talk to Mrs Lomar yourself, but that's what I got from her. She's sure she's never seen him before this.'

'I see. Has anyone made contact with Mrs Morris' sister?'

'I didn't know she had one. Bill Clark takes care of that stuff. I'll find out. Hold on. He's still here.'

Palmer waited, wiping himself dry as he did.

'OK,' Wizner said coming on. 'Yes. He reached an Edith Zucker in Duluth.'

'That's the one.'

'She's on her way.'

'Have Clark arrange for me to meet with her,' Palmer said.

'Will do.'

'OK. Thanks. I'm heading over to Mrs Morris' apartment.'

'Now?'

'I believe this guy I'm looking for might have called from there just now. It's possible.'

'All right. I'll call you if I get anything more on this.'

'Thanks,' Palmer said, hung up and started to call Tucker.

'Palmer?' Tracy called from the bathroom.

'Let me talk with Tucker,' he replied.

'Wait,' she shouted as she shot up and out of the tub. She reached for a towel.

'What?'

'I'm coming along,' she shouted.

'Like hell you are,' he called back. 'Even if I let you, Tucker would blow a gasket.'

She came out of the bathroom with the towel wrapped around her.

'I'll wait in the car. How's that?'

'He won't like it. It's against regulations to take a civilian along on a homicide investigation, Tracy.'

'I'm not a civilian. I'm your ... girlfriend ... we're practically engaged,' she said and then added, 'I'm just waiting for you to get up enough nerve to ask.'

He stood frozen with the phone still in his hand. 'Are you kidding?'

'Do I look like someone kidding about that? I'm standing here naked, Palmer, and I just washed your back,' she said. 'In some Far Eastern countries that's the same as a marriage commitment.'

He smiled and then shook his head. 'Women and timing,' he said. 'Put the tape on pause. I'll be back in a few hours and we'll continue the discussion.'

She grimaced.

'Please,' he pleaded. 'I've got to move quickly.'

'OK, if you'd rather go chasing after a killer,' she said, dropped the towel and then sauntered toward the bedroom, her beautiful curvaceous body simmering.

He laughed and dialed out Tucker's number, shouting, 'That's unfair, Tracy Andersen, dirty pool, and might even be obstruction of justice or an attempt to do so.'

'I'm still waiting for those handcuffs,' she shouted back.

Tucker Browning's gruff hello sobered him quickly.

'If you're undressed, dress. I'll be by in fifteen,' Palmer said.

'I knew it was you. I just knew it. Why are you coming around?'

'We're going back to Ceil Morris' apartment.' He described Wizner's first call.

'Broke down the door? Maybe he thought the old lady had more money stashed.'

'That's not the reason I'm calling you. He just called and it could very well have been from there.'

'Who just called?'

'Grandpa,' Palmer said.

'Who?'

'The grandpa/son. I gave her my card with my home number on the back, remember?'

Tucker was silent a long moment. 'How do you know it was him exactly?'

'He was screaming about his mother and justice, how he'll take care of it and how we should back off. I'll play it for you. Listen,' he said and put the receiver by the answering machine speaker.

'Well?' he asked when it ended.

'Just don't tell me you had a premonition and that was why you gave her the telephone number,' Tucker said. 'I can take anything but that.'

Eight

The payphone from which he made the call to Palmer Dorian was in the rear of the restaurant between the men's and women's rest rooms. It was an upscale restaurant on the lower East side, just across from Jack Temple's law offices. He did not know where Temple lived or he would have gone directly there. He realized this was a very connected lawyer who would be far less accessible than Father Martin, but he thought he would have an opportunity to confront him in the garage below the building. He had slipped in to look it over. There were two driving lanes to enter, one for the tenants and one for guests. Both lanes had bars across them that lifted. The tenant would insert a card or punch in a code, but the guests would have to stop and sign in with the parking attendant. All of the parking spaces were clearly delineated and everywhere possible there were signs warning drivers not to invade them. There were however, designated spaces for guests and clients. In the center of the garage were the elevators.

He located the space reserved for Jack Temple. It was at the far right end of the garage. While he was looking it all over, he noticed a space between the wall and the ceiling just to the right of Temple's parking slot. It was big enough for him to slip into. He had slept in worse places.

Satisfied with his plan for confronting Jack Temple, he returned to the restaurant, this time to eat and have something to drink. It would be his first alcoholic beverage for more than three years. Before now, he hadn't had the desire.

After he had called the detective, he went into the men's room and once again was very pleased with what he saw reflected in the mirror. The deep wrinkles in his face were far less emphatic and the circles around his eyes were nowhere nearly as dark and as puffy. He had never thought himself a terribly handsome man, but he always believed he had a sexual magnetism because of his deep blue eyes and the way he could undress a woman with them. Many sophisticated women noticed it and most even blushed, but it didn't turn them off. They felt the animal lust in him and it awakened it in themselves.

What was even more important, perhaps, was his self-confidence when it came to women. He was smooth enough so that they weren't turned off by his arrogance. He used to think of it as passengers in a jet feeling secure because the pilot gave off an aura of experience and confidence. It was the same with patients of great doctors. Lovers were no different, especially women. They would rather be in the hands of someone who knew his way down the road of lust and pleasure. There was no stumbling around, blundering modesty and awkward moments to make them self-conscious about their own sexual appetite – not with him.

When he looked at himself now, saw the rejuvenation taking place, he dared to hope that he would soon return to that world of Casanova, that he would once again be a player, strut and maneuver through the glitz and glamour of those expensive watering holes where beautiful women came to feed. He could close his eyes and imagine them all turning his way, smiling to themselves, nodding, wetting their lips, crossing and uncrossing their legs, palpitations starting to pump up the surface of their complexions until they blushed with desire.

All because of him.

I'm coming back, he thought. Beware female America.

He laughed to himself and went out to the restaurant, to his booth. He had only a few hundred left, but it was enough for now. He would have lots more by tomorrow, he thought. He began with an Irish whiskey on the rocks, then a Caesar salad and a New York strip steak. It came with creamed spinach and mash potatoes. Just as he had done in the coffee shop at breakfast, which now seemed like days and days ago, he wiped the plate clean with a piece of bread and then ordered the ice-cream mud pie for dessert. The waitress was amused at his ravenous appetite.

'Are you always this hungry?' she asked him once he'd cleaned up every drop of his dessert.

He looked up at her, actually looked at her for the first time. His mind had been focused entirely on the food.

A trained monkey could have brought it to him and he wouldn't have noticed.

She couldn't be more than twenty-four, twenty-five, he thought. Her hips were a bit wide, but she had an ample bosom and he liked her neck. He was always that way when it came to women. He was always looking at their necks, even before he looked at their breasts, legs or asses. Maybe he was a frustrated vampire after all, but in his mind's eye, he could see himself sucking, nibbling and kissing those necks first. He even liked the base of this girl's throat. It was sexy.

He smiled and sat back, spreading his arm over the top of the seat.

'I've been on this stupid diet,' he told her. 'Tonight, I decided to toss it.'

'You certainly did,' she said laughing. Then she grew serious. 'That's why I don't believe in diets myself. You follow some stupid regime and lose five, eight pounds and then go back to the way you were and in days, regain it. It's better just to eat in moderation and exercise. I know,' she added quickly, 'don't say it. I can use some moderation and exercise.'

'Hey, I wasn't thinking that at all. I was thinking how wise you are for your age.' She blushed. 'Shirley,' he added nodding at her name tag.

'Thank you. Can I get you anything else? More coffee?'

'Yeah, maybe more coffee,' he said. 'Thanks.'

She took his cleaned dish and walked back to the kitchen.

She's putting a little extra into that wiggle, he thought. They do it subconsciously after they get compliments. It wakes some sleeping beast in them. He loved analyzing women because he was confident that he really had an understanding of them. He thought of them almost as another species. The difference was just too great. Everything they did came from a different place. He doubted that they saw anything in the world the same way as men did.

Thinking these deeper thoughts suddenly caused him to wonder about something. Maybe, he had gained wisdom as quickly as he had developed gray hair, deeper wrinkles and all the rest. Wow. He had reached into that cave of wealth right under the nose of the dragon and plucked out some choice realizations, things that took other people decades to understand. Why shouldn't he have gained something good from all this? He deserved it.

Shirley returned with a fresh cup of coffee. When she leaned over to place it on the table, he could smell her body. It was a little disguised by her cologne, but that cologne had worn off enough for him to capture not her sweat so much as her identifying scent. Everyone had a different scent. Dogs proved that.

Another wild idea came rushing into his thoughts. What if as he was returning, rejuvenating, he was developing sharper senses? What if he was eating like this because he could taste food better than most people? What if he could see, hear, feel, smell better than most people now? What if he was a real Superman in a way? Imagine what a lover he could be.

He was smiling so deeply, it brought a smile to Shirley's face, too.

'You look pretty happy,' she said.

'Yeah. I was just thinking how lucky I am to be alive and kicking.'

She laughed. 'Why? Did you have some sort of close call recently?'

'You know, I did,' he said. He sipped some coffee. 'I nearly gave up on life. But I'm coming back,' he declared. 'And coming back strong.'

She laughed again.

'Are you engaged, married, involved with anyone?' he asked.

'Sorta,' she replied.

'Sorta married?'

'Sorta involved.'

'Well, get it sorted out,' he said and laughed. She just held her smile. 'Tell you what. I've got some very important business to do tomorrow. Maybe I'll come by again. If it works out like I think it will, you can celebrate with me. I'll take you to a restaurant that is four times as expensive as this one. Bet your sorta boyfriend won't.'

She lost her smile.

'He will when he can,' she said. 'I don't just go out with anyone who comes in. I'm sorry.'

Her unexpected response deflated him so quickly, he thought he had actually shrunk in the seat. What happened to that overwhelming effect he had on women?

'Hey, I didn't mean nothin',' he replied. 'I was just trying to be nice.'

'It's all right. I wish you lots of luck,' she said, tore out the bill and put it on the table. She flashed him a plastic smile and sauntered off, not wiggling at all.

His food seemed to harden in his stomach.

His mood did a flip-flop. What if these changes were temporary? What if he would degenerate again? Maybe there was nothing unusual about all this and they expected it. What if he would have not run away? Would they have delivered what they had promised? His mind reeled about in confusion for a few moments until he settled down and convinced himself they were not expecting this. They did not want him to survive. Remember Father Martin's face. If this were anticipated, he wouldn't have had that reaction. No second thoughts, he told himself. Keep going.

He pealed off the cash to pay his bill and then, now out of spite, he left Shirley a dollar tip. She had no right to turn on him like that and make him feel inadequate. Take a dollar. See how adequate that makes you feel, smartass, he thought as he rose and walked out without so much as glancing in her direction.

He walked for a while to calm himself and then he made a sharp turn, crossed the street and slipped into the parking garage. He started toward Temple's parking space when he heard the distinct sound of the elevator and pressed himself against the wall to watch and wait. Who was here this time of night? The door opened and a custodian stepped out. He started toward a small pickup truck that had print on the outside of the doors advertising custodial services.

Sure, he thought, the janitor. He would work at night. The janitor! He realized and sprung off the wall. The janitor didn't hear him despite the echo of footsteps. He probably imagined them to be his own. Who else would be here? Just as he reached his truck, Bradley stepped up beside him and put his knife to his throat.

The janitor, a short, somewhat plump, nearly bald man, gasped and froze.

'Easy, Mr Clean,' Bradley whispered in his ear. 'If you're good, you'll live.'

'What do you want?' the janitor managed, his voice squeaking with terror.

'I want keys.'

'Keys?'

'I want the keys to Jack Temple's law offices.'

He pressed the knife hard enough to actually cut the custodian's skin. The blood trickled on to the blade and then Bradley lifted the blade to show him. He couldn't see from behind, but the man's eyes literally bulged with fear. He nodded his head.

'Here,' he said, reaching into his deep overall pockets to produce a ring of keys.

'Hold them up and show me which one opens Temple's office doors. Go on.'

He held them up and illustrated that the keys were marked with tags. Temple's was obvious. There were three keys so Bradley imagined one opened the inner or private office. He took the ring from the custodian.

'OK, where are the keys to the truck?'

The custodian handed them to him quickly.

'Good. Now let's go around to the passenger's side of the truck,' he ordered.

They moved almost comically with the janitor taking small, careful steps and Bradley pressing against him and keeping the knife against his throat.

When they got there, he told the janitor to open the door. He did.

'OK, you get in first,' Bradley said and he started to do just that when Bradley slit his throat and then pushed him on to the seat.

While the man gagged on his own blood, Bradley calmly walked around the truck to the driver's side and got in. He looked down at him. The man's body shuddered and jerked about for a few more moments before growing still.

Bradley started the truck, backed up and drove out of the garage.

Couldn't leave the truck there, he thought. It would stir curiosity in the morning.

He drove until he found a relatively quiet side street and then parked the truck in the first spot he found. He pushed the custodian's body to the floor so it wouldn't be immediately obvious. Then he got out and started his walk back to the garage, the ring of keys jingling in his hands, the smile widening on his face.

Someone up there likes me, he thought and laughed aloud at his good fortune.

With their guns drawn, both Tucker and Palmer approached Ceil Morris' apartment. They listened outside the door for a few moments and then made their entrance. A quick perusal revealed the apartment was unoccupied.

Tucker looked back at the apartment door and whistled when he inspected the damage.

'Determined son of a bitch, wasn't he?'

Mrs Lomar, whom they had buzzed to get in, came out of her apartment to join them.

'Thanks for agreeing to see us, Mrs Lomar,' Palmer said immediately and handed her one of his cards.

She looked past him into the apartment. 'Did he steal anything?'

'We're not sure yet,' Palmer said.

'Do you know if she had anything of real value in here?' Tucker asked stepping up. 'I'm Detective Browning,' he said quickly.

'Ceil? She had less than me and I have nothing.' Mrs Lomar replied. 'Of course,' she added, 'you never know what someone might have buried in an old shoe box or something. A cousin of mine died and we thought she was penniless, but she had hoarded nearly fifty thousand dollars in a collection of antique Chinese vases. It was almost missed, but my sister, whose nosey enough to look in your ears, discovered it. Imagine?'

Palmer reached into his jacket pocket and produced the picture he had of Bradley Morris, the one from the correctional facility folder.

'Was this the man?'

She shook her head. 'No, he was older.'

'He didn't resemble him? In any way?' Tucker pursued.

She looked at the picture again. 'Maybe a little,' she admitted. 'Could be his brother, I suppose.'

'I know you've described the man to the detectives from

the robbery division, but could you tell us again exactly what
he looked like.'

She shrugged. 'Exactly? I didn't look at him long. I can
tell you he was in a very nice suit and an expensive looking
pair of shoes. He had gray hair very nicely styled, clean
shaven. I couldn't say how old he was, but I assure you it
made no sense for him to say he was Ceil Morris' son. I
know she was in her fifties and he looked at least as old as
that.'

'How old?'

'Maybe fifty, fifty-five.'

'Not older?'

'It's not easy to tell someone's age, you know,' she said
defensively. 'Some people age nicely. My sister's husband is
nearly eighty-one, but you would think he was no more than
seventy. He still has a full head of hair!'

'What about this man's hair?'

'It wasn't as full as my brother-in-law's. I can tell you that.'

'Could he have been made up to look older?' Palmer asked.
'Look at this photo again, please. Could this be the man made
to look older?'

She looked at him as if he was asking a nutty question.
'You mean like in a play or a movie?'

'Yes.'

She shrugged. 'I didn't get as close to him as I am to you
so I can't swear to anything like that. I didn't like looking at
him. He didn't have nice eyes. They made me nervous.'

'Can you remember exactly what he said?' Tucker asked.

'When I first saw him, and I saw the door and what he had
done, he said, he was worried about his mother. I'm sure he
said that, but when I asked him and told him I thought he said
he was her son, he looked like he was in a panic and said no,
he didn't say that. But he did,' she insisted. 'He must be a
nutcase. You think he might come back?'

Tucker looked at Palmer and then said, 'If you do see him
again, you should call us immediately.'

'Oh, don't worry about that,' she replied. 'I certainly
wouldn't hesitate.'

'Thank you for your help,' Palmer said.

'I didn't do much,' she said. 'Except run into a crazy man.'

They watched her walk back to her apartment.

'She might be the only one who knows what's going on here,' Tucker said. 'Can we go home now?'

'So what do you make of the perp's message to me, this comment that he is sorting out justice here and we should leave him be?' Palmer asked Tucker as they drove off.

'I go back to the old lady's comment. We're dealing with some nutcase.' He paused and looked at Palmer. 'You don't think he killed the cab driver in the name of some wild justice, do you?'

'No, that was probably a killing during a robbery and to keep him from being quickly identified. I do believe he didn't expect his mother to turn him in.'

'If she really was his mother, which I still strongly doubt, Palmer, she didn't exactly turn him in. She wanted us first to . . .'

'Punish those who had done him harm,' Palmer said, smiling. 'The realization she was robbed wasn't until later and she didn't actually seek to press charges against him. That was us sending Wizner there.'

'So how does Father Martin fit into this?'

'He's blaming or blamed him for something,' Palmer said.

'Look. As I said, I haven't bought into the idea that this is somehow Bradley Morris, Palmer. We have only the testimony of a woman who was quite disturbed and the fact that he's using Bradley Morris' name.'

'And the fact that the doctor who signed his death certificate at the prison was apparently murdered.'

'I admit that looks suspicious, but in the end that could turn out to be just be a hit-and-run.'

'What about Watson's heart attack brought on by a meth overdose?'

'We don't know if the guy was or was not a user. It doesn't make sense to us, but so much of what we see in this world we investigate doesn't,' Tucker said. 'Now that I hear this old lady's testimony, the idea that another con took on Bradley Morris' identity is making more and more sense to me. Ceil Morris wanted to believe he was her son. It's like that scene in *Catch 22*, remember, when those parents are brought in to see their dying son for the last time and it's not their dying son, but they accept him as so. No parent likes to face a child's passing.'

'Even . . .'

'Even if she buried him herself, yes.'

'OK,' Palmer said. 'I'll back off. Let's wait to see what we learn tomorrow.'

'There is a God after all,' Tucker cried. Palmer laughed. 'Get some sleep, Palmer,' he told him when Palmer dropped him off.

'I'll try.'

Tucker held the door open and then smiled. 'Got company?'

'Figure it out. You're a detective,' Palmer said.

Tucker laughed again and closed the door.

When Palmer returned to his apartment, he found Tracy waiting in his bed, but the toll was first he had to give her every little detail.

Then, and only then, did she agree to make love.

He thought it well worth the price.

Nine

Mrs Goodman gave Simon his freshly squeezed orange juice, his fresh coffee and his poached egg on whole wheat toast. She moved about silently. He kept his eyes on her every gesture and look, waiting for some sign that she anticipated his imminent demise. He had a suspicion that she would know what Mr Dover intended to do with him before he did. Paranoia came with the territory. You couldn't be part of a clandestine operation without being skeptical and leery. It was merely self-defense.

After breakfast, Simon went into his office, spread the lab reports in front of him on his desk and gazed at the numbers. In his mind's eye, he saw a graph that was twisting and spinning, tangling up like some tornado and in the process destroying his dream. He looked nervously at the clock. Mr Dover would be here any moment. He had to come up with logical, rational explanations. Regardless of all this confusion, he was on the verge of creating this great program. Despite the results with some specimens whereby their age was accelerated, and now this unexpected strong resurrection of some immune systems, he was still very confident of his success. It was just a matter of adjusting here, tweaking there. Hell, the inventor of the steam engine went through a development process with failures along the way, didn't he? Any inventor did.

He realized that even though he was doing a good job convincing himself, he wasn't sure he would be as successful with Mr Dover. By the time he was buzzed by security and informed of Dover's arrival, beads of sweat had soaked his forehead and hair. He rose quickly, went to his bathroom to straighten up and quickly dab cold water on his face. It wouldn't be good to appear nervous.

'I've got to convince him we'll be OK,' he told his image

in the mirror. 'I just need more time. I'll reassure him I'm close.'

He thought he heard his image say, You have already assured him that it was a nearly perfected process. You're not dealing with just any gullible entrepreneur.

He sucked in his breath and steeled himself nevertheless, forming his best smile like someone who had put on a mask. For a moment he just gazed out of his bathroom window like one of his inmate specimens gazing out at freedom. Outside, a roof of gray bruised clouds hovered in globs that looked like small hernias. It was not a good omen, not that he believed in omens much. He simply hated overcast skies with a passion and like someone having a tantrum, he would shut his blinds and curtains and refuse to look outside until there was some blue somewhere.

The sound of voices and his office door opening shattered his musings. His thoughts rained down like fragments of some precious crystal and he hurried out of the bathroom. Mr Dover wasn't alone. The man with him was quite recognizable. He was Senator Hastings who had just recently become chairman of the Senate Judiciary Committee.

Tall and lean with light blond hair that turned a pale yellow shade wherever there were gray strands invading, Dover had a firmness in his posture that suggested a spine literally made of iron. He had a military air bathed in self-confidence and neither moved nor spoke with the slightest hint of hesitation. And yet, he bore an uncanny resemblance to Jimmy Stewart and could at times look disarmingly soft and sweet, even as innocent as a Mr Smith who came to Washington.

Senator Hastings, however, had nothing contradictory either in his demeanor or voice. He was gruff, arrogant and impatient. Stout with the promise of soon-to-be thicker and puffier jowls in his round face, he had the habit of lifting the left corner of his thick-lipped mouth higher than his right when he spoke, especially when he spoke condescendingly or angrily. From what Simon had seen of him on television, the man rarely shouted. He spoke with a low growl when he was upset and leaned over his part of the senate chamber dais with his palms down as if he were about to pounce.

Unlike men who tried to compensate for lost hair, Senator Hastings kept his remaining hair short. From a distance, the black stubble looked like it was painted over his temples and down the back of his head with a shiny naked top that resembled a small pale white cap.

'Mr Dover,' Simon said nodding.

'Of course, you know Senator Hastings, Dr Oakland,' Dover said in response.

'Yes. Welcome,' Simon said and gingerly made his way to his desk, half-wondering if it was presumptuous of him to take that seat and seem more important. However, he was more important, he told himself and did it anyway. 'It's an honor to meet you, Senator Hastings,' he added after he sat. 'Please, have a seat, gentlemen. Should I order something to drink, coffee? Some Danish?'

'This isn't a social visit,' Dover said. He indicated the sofa to Hastings and Hastings sat, but Dover remained standing as if he wanted to have the symbolic posture of lording it over Simon.

'Oh, yes . . . I just thought . . .'

'You know that it was always our intention to involve the judicial branch of our federal government in this program,' Dover said, nodding at Hastings and ignoring Simon. 'Inevitably, there would be the questions hovering about civil liberties, due process, cruel and unusual punishment and the like. We don't, as you scientists do, work in a vacuum, Dr Oakland.'

'Oh, I understand,' Simon said. Despite the height of his chair, he felt like he was sinking. 'Sure. Of course. That's your area entirely, Mr Dover. I wouldn't dream of commenting or suggesting or—'

'Senator Hastings was recently informed of our research and our program,' Dover interrupted.

'Vaguely,' Senator Hastings said. Simon thought he growled it.

'Yes, well we're here to change that. I explained we had something of a glitch going on and Senator Hastings thought he should personally be on top of everything now. A great many people who came to this before he became chairman of the judicial committee have made commitments to this project and want those commitments realized and protected.'

Simon nodded, looked at Hastings who was staring at him so hard, it gave him a chill, and then Simon leaned forward to say, 'Absolutely. I'll do whatever I can. I'm sure I can explain everything to everyone's satisfaction.'

'Before you begin,' Senator Hastings said, 'I want you to know I once told someone who was bullshitting the judiciary committee with a long, complicated explanation of a genuine fuck up that one of my favorite authors, Kurt Vonnegut, wrote in a novel, if you can't explain what you're doing so a nine-year-old would understand it, you're probably a charlatan. Let's see if you're a charlatan, Dr Oakland.'

He sat back, folding his hands on his stomach.

Simon looked at Mr Dover. 'I don't understand.'

'What's to understand? Senator Hastings would like you to explain what the hell you're doing and what you've done and what's happened, Dr Oakland, and in such a way that a non-scientist can understand. I hope I don't have to translate everything for you.'

'No, I'm sorry. Sure. Of course.'

Dover sat back and then assumed his own senatorial demeanor.

'I have always been intrigued with the aging process living things experience. I have done some interesting and innovative work in the field. In fact, I don't think I'm being immodest by saying I'm recognized as an expert in the subject.'

'Good for you,' Hasting said out of the corner of his mouth.

'Yes, well . . . to explain . . . there is a strange and rare human disease called Progeria, and although it does not actually reproduce the pattern of aging, an accelerated aging process occurs. Perhaps you have seen victims of the disease or pictures of them, children who look like they're ninety-year-olds when they are no more than six or seven? Their life span is usually no longer than fifteen years.'

'I never heard of it,' Senator Hastings said sharply.

'Well, as I said, it's rare, but very dramatic.'

'What's that have to do with any of this?'

'Well, let's think of aging as the loss of cells, nerve cells, brain cells, cells dying. The body stops dividing and repro-ducing them. Human beings normally have fifty divisions and then die, chickens about twenty-four, a mouse fourteen to twenty-eight. In the long-lived Galapagos tortoise, cells will undergo ninety to 125 doublings. This victim of Progeria I described will have about ten. So, helping the body improve on the doublings could extend life and certainly youth.'

He paused and looked at Mr Dover. 'Is that simple enough? I could go deeper into the genetics, if you like.'

'Just go on Dr Oakland. We have lots to do here.'

'Yes, of course. Well, theorizing about how to extend the aging process to keep us younger led to the obvious reversal: accelerating aging such as we see with Progeria. In short, simply reducing the ability of the body to double its cells. I had done so successfully with a number of specimens. I was having a philosophical discussion about it with associates of Mr Dover when the proposition was presented.'

'Yes, the proposition,' Hasting said. 'I'd like us all to be on the same page. Let's get into that. Exactly what is the proposition as you see it, Dr Oakland?'

'Well, it was put more into a question first. When you think of it on the surface, who would want to accelerate aging? How could that in any way benefit anyone? I forget exactly who it was . . . maybe you recall, Mr Dover, but someone than made the suggestion that the prison system would benefit, the overburdened prison system, I might add.

'Philosophically or morally, the issue was how do you relieve the prison system, lessen the population, and still be sure those released have paid their debt to society? Too many prisoners are being paroled too soon because there is simply no room, the costs are too high—'

'You don't have to tell me about that,' Hastings interrupted. 'I have a lot to say about the budget for federal penitentiaries.'

'Right. Then came the "what if" question . . . I love "what if" questions,' Simon said smiling. 'They have the effect of stimulating my creative juices.'

'Good for you,' Mr Dover said. Simon thought he was giving him a compliment until he added, 'Get to the fucking point.'

'Sorry. I innocently asked, what if prisoners who were sentenced to ten, fifteen, twenty years could be aged ten, fifteen, twenty years practically overnight? They're going to be that age anyway by the time they get released, unless they had some parole of course. The ones who most likely won't be paroled are really the ones we're concentrating on at the moment. They are the most apt to volunteer. For obvious reasons,' he added.

Both men stared at him silently. He squirmed a bit and smiled. 'At the time I didn't know it, but I had intrigued some people who eventually reached Mr Dover. He and I met. I reviewed my progress with the research and how I had successfully accelerated aging with rats and a pig.'

'A pig?' Hastings asked.

'Oh yes. A pig is important because it resembles us humans . . . its heart is about the same size and pig valves are being used in human transplants as we speak. Bottom line was, I was successful in acceleration of aging and could even duplicate the actual time passed . . . how much the specimen would or should age in five years, ten years, twenty years.

'Think of how we could redefine human punishment,' Simon said visibly excited with his own explanation. 'It can't be cruel and unusual if it will happen anyway, right? The burden, however, is lifted from society financially, supporting the prison system,' he said and turned to a pamphlet on his desk. He flipped the pages quickly. 'Currently, it's estimated we're spending close to forty-five billion a year to maintain the nation's state correctional facilities and I don't have to tell you, Senator, that those costs are rising daily.'

'No, you don't have to tell me,' Hastings said dryly. 'I've already made that point.'

'Yes. Well, it doesn't take a rocket scientist to see that anyone responsible for such an innovation as I'm proposing and developing would be lauded worldwide, whether he be the scientist, the entrepreneur who eventually patents the process and owns it –' Simon said nodding at Dover – 'or the politician who had the vision to encourage the research.'

Simon sat back. He had made this case many times before to people Mr Dover had brought to him, and he could see from Dover's expression that he was doing well with it again.

'Go on,' Hastings said glancing at Dover and then turning back to Simon, who was tempted to sarcastically ask, How am I doing?

'Mr Dover was kind enough to get us the initial necessary financing for this clinic, my research. He found some human specimens for me.'

'Specimens?' Hasting asked grimacing. 'What the hell does that mean?'

'Homeless, mentally ill,' Dover explained.

'Oh. They were still alive then, living specimens as you call them,' Hastings asked.

'Yes. I'm sorry. I just think in scientific terms,' Simon said.

'Um,' Hasting muttered, but didn't look happy about it.

'It was slow going at first, especially because of the heart failures, but eventually I began to have remarkable success, charting my progress against substantial medical touchstones for human aging, without losing the specimen – the patient – and finally I believed we were ready to try our innovation on an actual convict.'

'And?' Hastings demanded.

'He was sentenced to forty years and was only thirty-eight at the time. Not a promising projection.'

'What did this convict do? His crime?'

'He was an enforcer for a drug lord,' Mr Dover said.

'And he agreed to this experiment?'

'A number of convicts submit themselves to experimental procedures in return for reduced prison sentences, as you know,' Simon said. 'This was no different except we were arranging for him to go into the federal identity protection program. He was out there with a new identity and approximately twenty years older, which was our compromise in negotiations. We had a crack team negotiating with them as well as Mr Dover and myself. However, I understand this arrangement was reversed today,' he added and looked at Dover.

'And you know why, too?'

'Why wasn't I called to do the evaluation?' he fired back, surprised at his own courage and aggressiveness.

'I wanted someone who had a little less of a stake in the matter,' Dover replied without hesitation.

'I don't know what you're talking about now, but how the hell did you get this all past Senator Jackson, Henry?' Senator Hastings asked Dover.

'We slipped under the radar when we went to the CIA,' Dover said.

'CIA?'

'The CIA was thinking of Dr Oakland's work in other terms . . . a terrific means of, quote, humane torture to get information. To see yourself age five years, ten, might stimulate a quicker submission, especially if there was some vague promise of reversal.'

Hastings spun on Simon. 'Is there?'

Simon looked at Dover and sank again in his seat.

'That's partly why we're here,' Dover muttered.

'Not intentionally,' Simon said. 'But to use Mr Dover's term, there is apparently a glitch with some specimens, I mean volunteers.'

'Which means?'

'Their immune systems are stronger than I had anticipated. So much is genetic, you see,' he added quickly. 'So . . .'

'And? What does that mean exactly . . . to a nine-year-old?'

'Well, They're battling back, returning to their actual chronological age.'

'You mean you made a deal with a convict, aged the bastard, let him out, and now he's getting younger?'

'We didn't exactly expect it because some of the others, actually all but one of the others, had aged too quickly, and beyond my expectations,' Simon said. 'Ten years became twenty, thirty. The last three died of old age in fact, so we thought we just had to work on tweaking the process and . . .'

'But these others, the ones who aged too much?'

'Well, once we saw what was happening, we aborted the process with them.'

'And aborted them,' Dover added dryly. 'Except for one who got passed us or Dr Oakland.'

'Well, he had aged too quickly and was rapidly approaching expiration as were the others, so I assumed . . .'

'So he went into a reversal, too, got younger?'

'It would seem so,' Simon said reluctantly.

'How young will he get?'

'Oh, not any younger than he was, if that.'

Hastings nodded and sat back, shaking his head. 'Well, there goes your "punishment still fits the crime" theory,' he said. He looked at Dover. 'You better be sure to abort him as well. Get him back from the identity protection agency.'

'I'm afraid it's looking like a little bit more than just that,' Mr Dover said. Simon looked up sharply. 'As Dr Oakland said, this one man was on his deathbed when the reversal started. He never entered the program on the outside.'

'Meaning?'

'I mean he's out there,' Dover said.

'Out there?' He glanced at the window as if they could all look out and see Bradley Morris looking up at them defiantly. 'Well, how did he get out there?'

'He escaped from the clinic,' Simon said. 'No one anticipated it because he was aged into his eighties and dying. I was simply keeping him alive to learn more and then . . .'

'And then he apparently got up and walked out,' Dover said.

'Amazing,' Hastings muttered nodding.

'He's understandably angry about what was done to him,' Dover added.

'I imagine so. And?' Hastings nearly shouted, his face getting red.

'He's coming after those who, shall we say, convinced him to take the deal.'

'How do you know that?' Hastings asked.

'He's killed Thomas Martin.'

'Father Martin?' Simon asked first. He hadn't known. Dover nodded.

'Why did he kill a priest?' Senator Hastings asked. 'How was he involved in this?'

'We all thought when the time came, it would be wise to have the religious element on our side. We began with Father Martin in NYC who got permission from the Vatican to co-operate with the program. He was already visiting convicts on a regular basis in a program he had initiated and was managing. We thought it made sense to bring him into it,' Dover explained.

'Killed a priest,' Hastings muttered. He looked up sharply. 'You have a lot of holes to plug up here, Henry. We can't let this get out.'

'I'm on it.'

'I'm sure the CIA is there to help bring this guy back.'

'Well . . .'

Hastings squinted at Dover. 'You haven't told them any of the bad news, have you?' He asked smiling slyly.

'Not yet. If we can plug this up ourselves . . . it's good to have them working with us, on our side, especially when it comes to financing, arrangements.'

'Um. What about this other convict, the one in the identity program?'

'He was doing well, but . . .' Simon began. He looked at Dover.

'I was nervous about him so I had him brought in and evaluated. He's creeping back,' Dover said.

'Creeping back? You mean, getting younger, too?'

'Yes.'

'Where is he now?'

'He's upstairs in the process of being terminated. To be sure there were no glitches. I thought I would leave him to trickle away so Simon here could look him over and see where the fuck up is. You will see that very quickly, will you not, Dr Oakland?' Dover asked, his voice dripping with threat.

'Yes, of course. I appreciate the opportunity,' Simon said moving his papers on his desk. 'In fact, I already have some new ideas about how to control this immune system problem and—'

'Let's keep this shut down until we're more than positive about it,' Senator Hastings said, interrupting again. 'But first, handle this situation with the one out there, Henry.'

'We will,' Dover said.

Senator Hastings nodded. 'Are you bullshitting us or do you really think you can make the corrections necessary and get rid of this glitch?'

'I do,' Simon said with as much confidence as he could manage.

'Well then, we'll revisit it all when you have something to show us. Get us into a ninety something success ratio. Aging too far around ten percent, or less, of the convict volunteers is something we can live with as long as they don't rebound and make us look stupid.'

'Exactly,' Dover said.

Hastings nodded and smiled at Simon.

'Actually, I'm rooting for you, Dr Oakland. I like the idea very much and I agree. It would be a most significant contribution toward the justice system . . . worldwide. Being part of something that significant would be a good thing, raise someone's positive public image as well as make a lot of money.'

'Turn him into a serious presidential candidate in fact,' Dover suggested.

Hastings nodded. 'Yes. It might.'

Simon took a deep breath and looked at the two men envisioning greater things for themselves. The good old personal ego, alive and well. Probably all scientific and social progress was tied to someone's personal agenda one way or another. This would be no different. They saw, envisioned, themselves as heroes with great financial gain as a consequence as well.

And all that depended on him.

He was still alive after all.

This time he would not fail.

Jack Temple's private office was about as luxurious as any office Bradley could imagine, and it wasn't only the glitter of the polished brass and the marble. All the furniture looked imported. He knew very little, if anything, about style, but he sensed an Old World European look to the sofas, the chairs, the tables and the desk. To complement that style, Temple had beautiful large oil paintings of recognizable European settings, such as the Eiffel Tower, the Tower of London, the Vatican, and the Spanish Steps in Rome, as well as a beautiful capture of the Venice canals. All the colors were vibrant.

The office itself looked more like a showcase than an actual working lawyer's headquarters. Nothing was out of place. Every piece of paper was placed neatly in its stack beside other documents. As far as he could see, the only imperfection in the entire setting was a small smudge on a window panel the custodian had missed.

'Reason enough to kill you,' Bradley muttered and laughed as he walked about the office, examining the unique looking paperweights that resembled famous statuary, the gold-plated pen and pencil holders, the embossed pewter bookends, anything and everything because it all looked imported and as valuable as anything else in the office.

The private bathroom was done in a rich, cream marble with specks of rose streaming through the sinks, the counters and the shower stall. The towels and washcloths were embellished with the letters JT in bold red letters and were neatly folded. Just like the office, the bathroom looked showcase perfect, right down to the new bar of scented soap in the soap dish.

For a moment he was simply envious. What a delightful experience it must be to come to this office every morning, he thought. The view of the city was breathtaking, especially at night. He could clearly see the Empire State Building. Lights from planes leaving and entering the New York area blinked against the background of twinkling stars. Anyone working here, controlling all this, would surely feel superior. It was the lair of arrogance, a place from which to dictate orders that would dramatically change lives, move fortunes, apply and bequeath power.

Why were some men chosen to have all this? Was it all just a matter of good luck, coincidence, timing, or was there truly a higher power that moved lives, careers, health, all of it in some divine design that human beings couldn't comprehend? Am I just as another pawn after all? he wondered. That idea reinforced his belief that he was being used to impose this justice on men who dared to tinker with that divine design. Why not? Why not think of himself as more than a mere angry, vengeful man turned loose? It helped him feel important and justify anything and everything he did.

He strutted across the office to another door and was surprised that it was locked. Running through the ring of keys, he located another that fit and opened the door expecting to see a closet perhaps with something even more valuable, but was surprised instead to see a bedroom that he thought suggested the Playboy mansion more than the Old World look of classic style in the office. There was a fluffy, thick white rugged floor and the furniture was all in laminated black and gold. The bedding was in black with large gold pillows and all the fixtures and lamps were a gaudy-looking brass. What clearly made it look like a sex den were the mirrors on the walls and ceiling.

From the pictures on Temple's desk, he concluded the lawyer was married. Bradley thought of this bedroom as being an indoor adultery court. Even if he wasn't married, it would be the web of a sexual predator. How many women had Jack Temple brought in here? Did he have clandestine cameras capturing the action? I would, Bradley thought, and looked at everything closely, searching for a hidden lens. He couldn't find any, but still believed it was there.

He paused. Of course, the bed was inviting, not for its sexual promises, but because he was simply exhausted. He returned to the office, got himself some cold bottled water, took a prolonged leak, washed his face with the scented soap, and then returned to the bedroom. He was sure to lock the door before he lowered himself to the incredibly inviting mattress and fluffy pillows. Sleeping on a cloud couldn't be any better, he thought. It was his last thought before sinking into his own pool of ink.

The sounds of muffled voices woke him. He sat up slowly, hesitant and worried that he would find his body had regressed, but instead, he was pleasantly surprised to discover the return of muscle. He was more limber, too and when he looked at himself in the wall mirror, he didn't see that aged, tired look anymore. He touched his skin. It was softer.

I'm coming back, he thought. I'm really coming back.

He rose and put his ear to the door to listen. He heard a female voice, pleasant, young, and then he heard Jack Temple. He was being given a cup of coffee and the newspaper. His day was beginning. He heard the secretary review his appointment schedule, including his conference calls, and then the office grew quiet until the phone rang and Temple answered with a pleasant, 'Hello, Henry'. Strangely then, he became silent, listening. Bradley heard him say, 'I see. Well, this isn't good, no. OK. I'll change some of my appointments and meet you at the Waldorf for lunch.'

Bradley then heard him end the call and call his private secretary. He dictated the changes he wanted made in his appointment schedule and she left. Very carefully and slowly, Bradley opened the door to peek out.

Jack Temple was at least six feet one, about Bradley's height. He had a John Kennedy classy style appearance, handsome, intelligent and reeking of self-confidence. His light brown hair was perfectly styled, not a single rebellious strand. Like his office, nothing was out of place on his body. Studying him in his seat of power, Bradley suddenly felt quite inadequate. What made him think he could sneak in here and intimidate such a man? When he rose out of that seat to confront him, he might simply blow him away. He thought he felt himself actually tremble for a moment.

But this was no time to turn back or run with his tail between his legs. He had come too far and had far yet to go. He dipped down into his well of ruthless means, his memories of the kills and the beatings he had successfully committed in the past, many of his victims being men at least as physically formidable as Temple. You just didn't fight fair, that's all. There was nothing polite or gentlemanly about his work.

He gazed about the bedroom and seized a small black onyx

statue of what he imagined represented Venus. This one actually had pubic hair carved into its pelvis and the breasts had
perfect, erect nipples. It was so erotic in fact that for a moment
he was distracted. He heard Temple make another phone call
to someone he called General.

'I have to tell you there has been a setback,' he began. 'You
know about Father Martin? His clerk called me. No, Dover
is not alerting you just yet. He has this idea he can recuperate
and perhaps continue, but I don't like the potential for exposure. I'm seeing him today. I'll call you afterward. Yes, get
on it. Right.'

Temple cradled the receiver and sat back thinking.

It's time, Bradley thought.

He let the bedroom door swing open a bit more. He watched
now through the cracked opening between the door and the
frame. The opening startled Temple who just sat there staring
for a moment. Then he rose slowly, paused, opened a drawer
and took out a thirty-eight snub nose pistol. He glanced at his
office door and came around the desk, moving slowly toward
the bedroom.

Bradley crouched like a wildcat preparing to lunge. Temple
pushed the door open wider and paused.

'If anyone's in here, you'd better show yourself,' he declared.

Bradley held his breath. He heard Temple take another
forward step and then move to his left and pull the door shut
to reveal anyone behind it. Bradley was surprised at his speed
and agility, but he timed it perfectly so that when he was
exposed, he was already in the air, swinging the statue and
striking Temple squarely on his forehead. The blow stunned
Temple and sent him back into the wall. Bradley slammed
the bedroom door closed as he took another step, seized the
pistol and twisted it out of Temple's weakened grip. He struck
him again on the top of the head and Temple literally sat,
barely able to retain consciousness.

Blood seeped out around the wound on his forehead and
soaked the surrounding skin. It began to trickle in a thin stream
down both sides of his nose and over his eyes. He blinked,
but didn't try to wipe it away. He had lost his coordination
for the moment and was as helpless as a puppet off its strings.
His arms just dangled at his sides.

Bradley crouched to look into his face. He held the pistol

in his left hand and the statue in his right. Temple opened and closed his mouth without speaking.

'Well, hello, counselor,' Bradley said. 'Remember me?'

Jack Temple finally managed to raise his right hand to his forehead. The sight of so much blood on his palm panicked him. He struggled to back away, but Bradley tapped him pretty hard on his right shoulder and stopped him from moving.

'Relax. This is just . . . what did you call it . . . a preliminary, exploratory meeting? Yes, it was something like that. The second time was when you had me sign those papers, right? Where are they? Did you burn them or what?'

Temple shook his head. 'You're making a mistake,' he managed.

'Won't be the first. After all, I ended up in prison, didn't I? You don't end up in there unless you make a mistake and get caught.'

'What do you want?'

'Start by telling me who General is,' Bradley said. 'I overheard you tell him about poor Father Martin.'

Temple didn't respond.

Bradley lifted the pistol and pointed it at Temple's face. Then he pulled back the hammer. 'You obviously know what I did to Father Martin. I'm not bluffing here. Old people like myself don't have much patience, Jack, so you'd better talk fast.'

'He runs the CIA,' Temple said. 'So you're making a mistake, a big mistake.'

'Ooooh,' Bradley said faking fear. 'I bet I'm in some danger now. How much money do you have here and don't bullshit me. If I'm not happy with your answer, I'll see no reason to waste time.'

'I have eight hundred in my wallet,' Temple told him.

Bradley put down the statue and reached into Temple's suit jacket to pull his wallet out of the inside pocket. He opened it with his one hand and looked at the bills.

'OK, good start. I bet you keep more here.'

'Bottom drawer on the left of my desk . . . there's an envelope with two thousand dollars in it. Take it and get out.'

'And the papers I signed?'

'I don't have them. Dover kept all that.'

'What do you know about what's happening to me? You just spoke with Mr Dover. What did he say?'

'The process is flawed. Some are aging too fast, too quickly, and some, like you, are rebounding unexpectedly.'

'Rebounding.' Bradley smiled. 'It's true then. What I felt is true. I'm getting better.'

'We don't know that. You might have other problems as a result. You had better get yourself back to the clinic, and fast,' Temple said.

'Yes, where is this clinic exactly?'

'You just wait. I'll make a call and get someone to pick you up.'

'Were you always a man of action, Jack? Always in control?'

'You had better do it. You could just drop dead.'

Regaining his composure, Temple pulled a handkerchief out of his pocket and began to dab his forehead. He then held his handkerchief against the wound.

'There are effects on your heart you don't even realize,' Temple added.

'You know, I really appreciate your concern for my welfare, Jack. You were just as convincing at the prison during those meetings.'

'It's better for everyone if you do what I tell you, especially for yourself. Don't be stupid. They'll find you eventually and where can you go anyway?'

'Well, I was thinking seriously of this Greek island. I have some friends there.' He looked around. 'How many women you have here, Jack? Ten, twenty, what?'

Temple didn't answer. He closed his eyes and took another breath.

'You record any of it? I bet you did.'

'If you're smart, you'll just go sit in my outer office. I'll make the call. They'll take care of you.'

'Yeah, I know they will.' He gripped the statue again and stood up.

'Just calm down,' Temple said. 'I'll fix things.'

He started to struggle to his feet.

'I'm sure you will, Jack,' Bradley said and swung the statue again. Temple's chin sagged. 'You'd fix me fine, you and your powerful friends.'

He swung it at least five more times, feeling Temple's skull crack and shatter. Then he kicked him over and caught his breath. He looked at the statue in his hand. 'What a terrific piece of ass,' he muttered and tossed it to the floor.

He straightened his jacket, wiped his hair back with his palms and went out to Temple's desk to look in the bottom left drawer. The envelope was there.

'What'dya know. You told the truth for once, Jack. Thanks.'

He pocketed the bills and then he returned to the bedroom door to lock it. After that he walked out of the office as calmly as possible. Jack Temple's secretary looked up surprised. He paused at her desk.

'Hi. Oh, Jack asked that he not be disturbed for a few hours. I'm Bradley Morris. Me and . . . what's her name . . . were in the bedroom. Now it's his turn. Thanks,' he added and walked out. He glanced back as he closed the door and saw the secretary staring with her mouth open.

'Careful,' he called back to her, 'or you'll catch flies.'

Laughing, he closed the door

I'm coming back, he thought, I'm really coming back.

Ten

Palmer recalled that Tucker was going to an early morning dentist appointment and would be at the precinct later than usual. He was at work early that morning mainly because Tracy had to be on her way early to a building site in Westchester. Beating Tucker to the precinct rarely happened, but it gave him an opportunity to get some calls made. The first call shocked him. He called the rectory where Father Martin had been murdered and a woman answered.

'This is Detective Dorian, NYPD. I'm looking for Gerald Spenser,' he said.

'Mr Spenser is no longer here,' she replied.

'What? Who is this?'

'I'm the housekeeper, Rosina Castillo.'

'What do you mean, Mr Spenser is no longer there?'

'He left very early this morning.'

'Where did he go?'

'I don't know. He didn't tell me. A car came for him and he left. He said he wouldn't be back, but . . .'

'But what?'

'He left some of his things and he didn't tell me what to do with them.'

'He didn't tell you where he was going and he didn't tell you what to do with his things?'

'That's right.'

'Are you sure he said he wouldn't be back?'

'I arrived just as he was leaving this morning. That was what he told me. He even wished me luck before he left and gave me a small bonus that he said Father Martin had always intended to give me.'

'Did he leave in a taxicab?'

'No. It was a black limousine. I imagine it was one of those car services, although there was another man beside the driver and they were both in suits. Neither man wore a driver's uniform.'

'He didn't say he was going to a new position in Pittsburgh?'

'No.'

'What did Mr Spenser leave behind? What sort of things?'

'Clothes, shoes, some of his toiletries and all of his books. He reads a lot.'

'Did you see what he took with him?'

'Just one small suitcase,' she said. 'Maybe he'll call or write to tell me where to send everything else. I guess he was just in a big hurry. A very big hurry,' she added.

'I'm sure that's a correct guess. Look, take down my number and call me if he gets in touch. This is police business so it's very important.' He dictated his number.

'It's all so terrible,' she said after writing the number. 'I feel like crying all the time I'm here now. Do you know when I can go in and clean up the living room? They still have tags and ribbons around the furniture.'

'Someone will be there to tell you,' Palmer said. 'Don't do anything until you are told.'

'I know,' she said. 'There was a murder in my family five years ago and we couldn't go into the house for weeks.'

He hung up and sat thinking. Then he made the second call, this one to the correctional facility in Woodbourne, and what he learned from this call made him so impatient, he practically leaped out of his chair the moment Tucker arrived.

'Man, you look raring to go,' Tucker said smiling. 'Someone boost your battery last night?'

'Something like that. How was your dental visit?'

'"I would rather be in Philadelphia." Isn't that on W.C. Fields' tombstone?'

Palmer laughed. 'Have a seat. I don't want you standing when I give you the news that will help round out your painful day.'

'Thanks for being considerate,' Tucker said sitting.

'First, Gerald Spenser left town without calling in the information we requested.'

'Left town? For how long?'

'The housekeeper said he told her he wasn't coming back. She doesn't know where he went and it sounds weird. He left most of his clothing and personal things. She said he left in a hurry.'

Tucker nodded, thinking. 'Well, maybe he headed for his new position in Pittsburgh. Maybe they moved up his starting date.'

'She didn't know, but she was adamant that he was leaving for good and he didn't leave a forwarding address. If it was his new position, why wouldn't he leave a forwarding address?'

'Yeah,' Tucker said nodding. 'That is strange. How did he leave?'

Palmer described the car and the driver and passenger.

'We'll have to get to someone in authority at the church to see what they know.'

'I've got a call in to Monsignor Di Bona.'

'OK. What else? You look like you're about to explode.'

'Since Gerald left without providing the information we asked him to provide, I called the correctional facility to get the dates and times of Father Martin's visits.'

'And?'

'There is no record of any Father Martin visits.'

'Recently?'

'No record, period. None, nada.'

'That's ridiculous. He had to sign in,' Tucker said. 'That's a maximum security penitentiary.' Palmer stared at him. 'Maybe someone just didn't look in the right place.'

'No, I was persistent. They checked and double-checked. I even had a brief conversation with the man temporarily assigned to serve as warden.' He looked at his notes. 'A Thomas Wilson. He got on the other line and checked as well and then reconfirmed what I was being told.'

'That's incredible. It's almost like someone is anticipating every move we make and cleaning things away before we get there.'

'Exactly. Just before you walked in, I took a shot at reaching that young Dr Friedman at the ER and he happened to be on duty. He said the meth diagnosis as cause of death for Watson was absolutely accurate. I've got Vince Marcus checking to see if the man had any drug history, although I would say that was pretty unlikely in light of whom and what he was.'

'Absolutely. He was either a brand new, stupid user or . . .'

'Or poisoned with it.'

'Why meth?'

'It can be ingested, disguised in food. As you know it can produce chest pains and hypertension which can result in cardiovascular collapse and death. Since Crowley was conveniently run over before we could question him about his examination of Watson, we don't have much else to go by, and I don't have much confidence in an investigation in a prison to determine who might have poisoned the warden.'

Tucker shook his head, a look of amazement on his face. 'When we began this, I thought we were in a weird enough case about a psychotic elderly guy. That would have been enough. Let's get an APB out on this Gerald Spenser.'

'Done.'

Palmer's phone rang. 'Dorian,' he said, looked at Tucker and then said, 'we'll be right there.' He cradled the receiver. 'Chief wants to see both of us right now.'

Tucker's eyebrows suddenly awoke. 'To what do we owe this invitation to the Papacy?' he asked.

Palmer smiled and stood. They walked to the office, knocked and entered.

Chief of Detectives Carl Foreman hovered over the papers on his desk like a convict protecting his food in the prison cafeteria. He had shoulders padded with deltoid muscles that strained his uniform shirt. Even though he wore a tie, he wore it loose, the collar button undone. Stubborn about refusing to acknowledge any changes in style, Foreman kept his hair cut military short, even when he began to thin out and have a receding forehead. He was fond of saying, 'I need only spend a second or two on my hair in the morning. I brush it with a washcloth, unlike you pussies who worry you don't resemble James Bond enough.'

On his office wall were the plaques and citations he had won in college as a champion prize fighter. He was a contender, in fact, for the USA Olympic boxing team.

He looked up.

The man has to have a face of granite, Palmer thought. His six o'clock shadow never lightened or darkened and his lips never quivered. They barely stretched when he smirked or smiled, which was rare. His eyes were pure marble with specks of gray in his brown pupils and his nose couldn't be straighter if the Creator used a level to design the way it sloped into hard nostrils. His cheekbones were as prominent as the jawbone. Everyone was reluctant to call him heavy or stout because there was a connotation of softness in that word that simply didn't exist in Foreman's body. He was hard all over. Palmer wondered if Foreman's wife thought she was being embraced by a statue, especially in bed.

'Tell me about this case you're on,' he said and sat back, his hands behind his head.

'It's not a short story,' Tucker warned him.

'Make it one,' Foreman said. 'Palmer?'

Palmer began with Ceil Morris' visit and the events that immediately followed. When he described their trip to Woodbourne, he made sure to add it was something they were doing on their own, after hours.

Foreman didn't change expression or say anything critical or sarcastic which encouraged Palmer. 'Go on,' he pressed.

Tucker took over and described what they had learned in Woodbourne and what had followed just this morning relating to Gerald Spenser and the prison.

'Give me that description the neighbor provided,' Foreman said and Palmer went through his notes.

For a long moment, Foreman just stared at them and thought.

'What's up, Chief?' Tucker finally asked.

'We have another brutal murder that looks associated,' Foreman said sitting forward.

'Who?' Palmer asked quickly. He was anticipating Mrs Lomar.

'Big time attorney, Jack Temple, was bludgeoned to death this morning. Another homicide, the killing of a custodian, was just discovered as well because his truck was parked in a tow-away zone. The custodian services Temple's building and offices. His keys were missing. He was killed exactly as was Father Martin and that taxicab driver – throat slit. It looks like the same type knife was used, too.

'Temple's secretary provided a description similar to the one you just gave me. However,' he added looking down at some notes he had written on a pad, 'she said he also told her his name. He wasn't shy about it.'

'Bradley Morris?' Tucker asked.

'That's it.'

'This is very weird now,' Palmer said.

Foreman raised his eyebrows. 'Oh, you find it weird?' he asked, his voice dry with sarcasm.

'No, listen, Chief, he was careful about not leaving his prints on the cab when he did the driver, right Tucker?'

'Forensics said they were wiped clean.'

'And then he was careful in Father Martin's to wipe the glass he used clean.'

'We lucked out with prints on an icon,' Tucker said. 'Even though as Palmer told you, we're having a problem locating Bradley Morris' prints on file. Wiped out of the FBI files, apparently.'

'He wouldn't know that, so he was careful about not being identified. He even denied being Bradley Morris when his mother's neighbor confronted him.'

'So why would he brag about who he is now?' Tucker asked.

'Unless he is feeling invulnerable,' Palmer said.

'Why would he?' Tucker asked.

Foreman looked from one to the other as if he were just an observer, listening.

'Delusions of grandeur,' Palmer suggested. 'Something's got him thinking he's above everything. He's moved pretty much at will so far and done whatever he set out to do.'

'These deaths, murders, seem quite unrelated,' Tucker mused. 'We need to find the connection.'

'Are you guys finished?' Foreman asked them.

They both looked at him as if they had just realized he was there.

'If you are, please indulge me by getting your asses up to Temple's office and then cover the forensic work on this custodian and his truck. I didn't mean to interrupt. It was quite intriguing.'

'We're on it, Chief,' Tucker said. He glanced at Palmer.

'What about these missing prints?' Palmer asked.

'I'll look into that myself, but the last resurrection was well into two thousand years ago, so I wouldn't worry about the actual Bradley Morris,' he said.

'Unless that's not Bradley Morris in the grave, Chief,' Palmer said.

'We're not getting an order to dig up a grave on the basis of the testimony of a dead woman and two coincidental, definitely unrelated, deaths, the doctor and warden.'

'Even though both deaths are suspicious?'

'Tucker, keep on point, will you,' Chief of Detectives Foreman said.

'I'll try, Chief,' Tucker said, 'but I'm slipping around a bit myself.'

Foreman shook his head and hovered around his paperwork as they left.

Gerald Spenser was surprised to hear directly from Henry Dover. Almost every time Mr Dover called Father Martin, he had a secretary call. In fact, Gerald couldn't remember ever hearing Henry Dover's voice. He did look out the window one time when Dover's limousine arrived for Father Martin and got what he would call a glimpse of the man sitting in the rear, waiting for Father Martin and extending his hand as the door was opened.

Dover began the call by offering condolences. He then told Gerald that he was afraid the murder of Father Martin was related to the work they had been doing. Although Gerald's knowledge of it was very limited, he understood it was something to be kept highly classified for the time being. The closest Father Martin came to revealing any details about this project was when he told him it would be the most significant alliance between science and religion to defeat Satan ever attempted.

'As you know, Gerald,' Father Martin would say, 'every sinner who redeems himself, frustrates Lucifer. Too often our poor sinners are denied that opportunity. I am enthusiastic about this project because it will give them that chance.'

Gerald wanted to ask more questions, to know more details, but Father Martin told him it was better for now if he didn't know any more.

'Not everyone will have the same view as this,' he explained. 'There will even be significant opposition within the Church itself. I have to protect those who have faith in me and my judgment. I'm sure you understand.'

He did and he didn't. He so wanted Father Martin to think of him as more than his clerk, his assistant. He wanted him to think of him more as a brother or a son, perhaps even a soul mate. Although he would deny it to himself, he was enthralled whenever Father Martin touched him, put his arm around him, or merely smiled warmly at him. Father Martin never knew it, but Gerald had actually gone out of town to a church in the suburbs to confess his 'unclean' thoughts about his mentor and himself.

'I have reason to believe you need my protection for a while, Mr Spenser,' Henry Dover said. 'Some things have occurred that lead me to believe this.'

'Oh, really? The police have been here so—'

'They have no idea what they're looking for, Gerald,' Henry Dover interrupted, now addressing him by his first name to get closer to him. 'They can't protect you.'

'You think he'll be back, this man who killed Father Martin?'

'I have no doubt he'll be back. He's on an insane rampage. You, being such a close confidant of Father Martin, will be seen as a target.'

'But why didn't he . . . try to harm me when he was here?'

Dover was silent a moment and then said, 'I didn't want to have to tell you this but I'm sure I can depend on your discretion.'

'Yes, of course.'

'Father Martin wanted to involve you more in this project. He wrote some things that I'm afraid have fallen into the killer's hands.'

'Involve me?'

'He was adamant about it, claiming you were his most trusted assistant.'

'Oh.'

'He went so far as to claim you and he were more like brothers.'

'He said that?'

'He did. I was moving toward approving your exposure to highly classified information. My associates agreed. We wanted Father Martin's full confidence and assistance. Anyway, Gerald, will you let me protect you until this is over? It won't be long. We are hot on the trail and expect to have a resolution in a matter of days.'

'Yes, of course. Thank you,' Gerald said and agreed to the arrangements immediately.

'You understand why you have to be absolutely discreet about it . . . no details to anyone.'

He did and he was ready. When the car arrived, he let only Father Martin's housekeeper know he was leaving and he had her convinced he was leaving for good, which was what Mr Dover wanted.

'If there's reason to believe you won't return, our demon, if I can be so bold as to call him that – I'm sure Father Martin would if he were still with us – our demon will give up on you.'

Gerald understood.

It was done as Mr Dover requested.

The men who picked him up were more efficient than friendly, he thought. They said little and he thought it was probably better that he said little himself. He didn't know how much they knew about the situation.

When they drove over the George Washington Bridge and headed toward the upstate New York area, he almost asked after their ultimate destination, but he wasn't sure they weren't told he already knew. He was simply afraid of stirring up any suspicions whatsoever and kept his mouth shut.

Eventually, they pulled into a rather modern building with a sign over the entrance that declared it to be the home of Classic Industries, whatever that meant. Maybe it was Mr Dover's company, he thought. The passenger in the front took his small suitcase for him.

'Come along, Mr Spenser,' the driver said and finally offered a smile.

He nodded and followed them into the building.

The lobby was dimly lit, but obviously pristine. The floor was a dark gray marble and there was a marble counter top to his right and an elevator on his left. On the counter top was a telephone. The driver lifted the receiver, looked at him and then simply said, 'We've arrived with Mr Spenser.'

He cradled the receiver and folded his arms.

'It'll be just a moment, Mr Spenser,' he said.

Gerald looked at the second man. Neither had offered their names, which he thought was some standard operational procedure. He straightened his tie, pulled down on his jacket sleeves and stood straighter, watching the elevator door.

It opened and Simon Oakland stepped out. Gerald couldn't help but widen his eyes at the sight of such a small man, who was maybe a few inches here and there beyond being a dwarf. He extended his puffy small hand.

'Mr Spenser, I'm Dr Oakland. Mr Dover told me to expect you, fill you in and make you comfortable. Please,' he said, reaching for Gerald's small suitcase, 'let me show you around.'

Gerald smiled and nodded. 'Oh, I can carry that,' he said.

'No problem. I need the exercise,' Simon said. He looked

like it was an effort to carry it, however. He led Gerald to the elevator and just before the doors closed, smiled at the two men and said, 'Thank you, gentlemen.'

They didn't reply. They were leaving even before the elevator doors closed.

'I'm sure you're just full of questions about everything,' Simon said. 'We'll go to my apartment and offices, have a little lunch, and I'll start explaining the project to you.'

'Thank you,' Gerald said.

'I know you've been through a very, very traumatic and difficult time, Mr Spenser. We all appreciate how you've handled yourself under the circumstances.'

'I'm still not over it, not by a long shot,' Gerald said.

'Nor would I be,' Simon told him as the doors opened. 'Nor would I be. Please,' he extended his hand and Gerald walked out and into Simon Oakland's office.

'Nice view,' Gerald said looking out the big windows at the landscape below.

'Yes, a perk for someone who has to spend so much of his time inside. Please, have a seat at the table.' He put Gerald's suitcase down. 'Let's have something to eat. You like turkey?'

'Yes.'

'Good. My housekeeper, Mrs Goodman, makes a wonderfully moist turkey sandwich. Would you like coffee or tea or a cold drink?'

'Something cold, yes.'

'Oh, we have fresh lemonade. Would that be OK?'

'Perfect, thank you,' Gerald said.

Simon lifted his phone at the desk and called their order in to Mrs Goodman. Then he joined Gerald at the desk.

'So, what do you know about our work, the work Father Martin supported?'

'Not very much, I'm afraid. I just know it involved prison inmates and it had something to do with redemption.'

'Oh, absolutely. Redemption,' Simon said. 'We've been working on a way to get them to that goal faster. Not brainwashing them,' he added quickly. 'Nothing like that. Father Martin wouldn't stand for such a thing anyway, I'm sure. The whole point is that the sinner had to willingly find his remorse and believe in redemption himself.'

'Yes.'

They turned as Mrs Goodman entered with a tray upon which there were two sandwiches, two glasses of lemonade and two dishes of coleslaw.

'Mrs Goodman makes the coleslaw herself, too,' Simon said as she put it on the table. 'She's another great perk for me,' he added.

Mrs Goodman glanced at him, not sure she liked being classified as a perk. He smiled at her nevertheless. She looked at Gerald and then left the office.

'Not the greatest personality,' Simon leaned over to whisper, 'but worth the sacrifice. She cooks and bakes and takes such good care of me, my mother would be jealous.' He smiled and reached for his sandwich. 'The lemonade is homemade, too. Oh, I said that.'

Gerald smiled. The sandwich did look good. He took a bite and nodded. 'Terrific.'

'Enjoy. You deserve some comfort and good food after what happened.'

Gerald drank some lemonade and nodded again. 'Haven't had such fresh lemonade since I sold it myself on a street corner when I was a little boy,' he told Simon, who laughed.

'Grew up in the country, did you?'

'Yes, in Connecticut, actually.'

'I was a city boy, which is why I do enjoy being out here,' Simon said. 'Even though I have little free time. This work is quite demanding.'

'What sort of a doctor are you?' Gerald asked, before biting into his sandwich and drinking his lemonade.

'I'm in research solely, pure research, although I could be a family physician. I specialize in the study of aging.'

'Aging?'

'Yes, aging is really a disease, you see. If you think of it that way, the way you should think of it, you can then think in terms of a cure.' Simon smiled and leaned in to whisper again. 'Some of my benefactors think I'm working on that solely and that someday soon I'll restore them to their youth.' He chuckled.

Gerald thought his eyes rolled and his face bubbled. He looked at the window and thought it had clouded up outside. Then he looked at the sandwich in his hand and suddenly felt a little nauseous.

Dr Oakland continued to talk, but his words ran into each other so that Gerald had difficulty understanding. In fact, they soon became more of a single, long note.

'I . . .' Gerald attempted to speak.

Dr Oakland nodded, smiled and ate the rest of his sandwich.

Gerald seemed to float over the table, and sink slowly to it like a balloon losing air. He didn't hit it hard. He actually lowered his forehead to it gently.

Simon ate his last bite and then rose and went to his phone.

'Mrs Randolph, send in the gurney please,' he said into the receiver. Then he returned to the table and wiped his mouth with his napkin.

The two attendants rolled the gurney in with Mrs Randolph following. They said nothing. They lifted Gerald and gently spread him over the gurney. One attendant began to roll it out and the other took the small suitcase.

'Get him prepared for the first-stage treatment,' Simon told Mrs Randolph. 'I'll be there in fifteen minutes.'

'Yes, Doctor,' Mrs Randolph said.

She followed the attendants out and closed the door. Simon went to the phone and called Mr Dover, who picked up on his cellphone just as he was being taken to the Waldorf.

'Don't screw up anything with this one, Simon,' Mr Dover said.

'Oh, I'll be extra careful from here on in, Mr Dover.'

'Umm,' Henry Dover said. 'So will we all, Simon. So will we all.'

Simon hung up and looked out the window. It was a nice view. He meant every word of it.

At least Mr Dover is being efficient, he thought, presenting me with another specimen rather than just eliminating it.

Waste not, want not.

No matter how far we progress, how many wonderful new things we create, how funny it is that the old adages still ring true.

Don't dilly dally, Simon, he told himself as he headed for the door, a rolling stone gathers no moss.

He laughed. It felt good. He had been so frightened earlier. Now, he felt he was in charge again.

Eleven

Palmer looked down at the battered body of Jack Temple. Despite what had been done to him, the dead man wore a grimace that resembled an insane smile. Perhaps, as his life was being beaten out of him, he realized the irony of being so well-off, powerful, seemingly completely protected and now so easily the victim of what looked increasingly like some madman with enough smarts to get into Jack Temple's private offices and pull off this crime. In the end Temple was just as vulnerable as some poor slob wandering the back streets at night in the city, prey for the parasites and leeches that bore some resemblance to mankind, or maybe personified the true evil nature lurking inside us all.

The CSI unit was completing their sweep. They had already lifted the prints from the small marble statue that had been used as a club and, through the miracle of computer technology, had matched them with the prints lifted from the icon in Father Martin's living room. It was the same man who now boldly declared himself to be Bradley Morris. It was as if he were challenging law enforcement, calling him at his home. He was daring them to catch him. But why pretend to be a dead man, a convicted felon confirmed murdered in prison and buried by his own mother? Why then go to her to pretend to be her resurrected, albeit aged son? Was she the only person he thought he could rob? And was that booty enough? Two thousand dollars? It just didn't make sense unless he was simply some loose canon, a true nutcase.

The link between the deaths of Dr Crowley, who had provided Bradley's death certificate, and the warden, who had signed the report of his murder in the penitentiary, with Father Martin, who had a spiritual program for the inmates in that penitentiary, was far more intriguing. Now, the question was, why Jack Temple?

Tucker was in the office sifting through papers, searching

for clues. Palmer returned to the outer office to speak to Temple's secretary who was now lying on the small settee, a cold washcloth over her eyes. He saw she was tall with the figure of a runway model. He pulled up a chair. She reached for the cloth and removed it to turn to him.

'I know this is quite a shock,' he began, 'but what you can recall now might be the best information we can gather. Can you give me any more detail about the man's description? You said he was well dressed?'

'Yes, although now that I think of it, his suit was quite wrinkled and creased. He looked like he had slept in it.'

'In that bedroom,' Palmer said.

'Maybe,' she said obviously not happy about referring to Jack Temple's sex pad.

'Let's take it slowly, top down. His hair. Visualize.'

'Messy. I mean, also looked like he had just got out bed, grayish with some dark brown on his temples, but thin.'

'You didn't see the color of his eyes?'

'No. I was in such shock seeing him at all.'

'Was he tall, as tall as Mr Temple for example?'

'Yes, at least six feet, although he had bad posture, rounded shoulders.'

'Is there any chance you saw something on his neck?'

'His neck . . . a dark spot. Like a . . . tattoo or something,' she said nodding.

'Do you know if Mr Temple had any contact with a priest in town named Father Martin?'

She started to shake her head and then stopped. 'Just a minute,' she said rising. She returned to her desk and looked at her call sheet. 'Yes. Day before yesterday there was a call from someone named Gerald Spenser. He said he was Father Martin's clerk and Mr Temple should call him immediately. It was left on our answering service.'

'Let me see that,' Palmer said joining her. She turned the book so he could read the time of the call. He saw it was right after he and Palmer had returned from Woodbourne and visited Gerald Spenser.

'Did Mr Temple call him back?'

'Not as far as I know, but he doesn't always make his calls through me. He has a direct personal line.'

'OK, this is helpful,' Palmer said. 'Thank you. If you

remember anything else about him, no matter how insignificant you might think, please call,' he said handing her his card.

She took it and looked down at her desk. She lowered her chin so quickly, he thought she might have fainted.

'You want someone to help you get home?' he asked.

'Home?' She looked up. 'I . . . there are people to call, things to do. I put all the incoming on the answering service. I'll have to get back to people.'

'Yes, but maybe not today.'

She nodded.

Palmer went into the office just as Tucker hung up the phone at Temple's desk. He quickly told him what Temple's secretary had revealed concerning Gerald Spenser.

'So, he knew Father Martin,' Palmer concluded.

'I knew that already,' Tucker said. He handed Palmer Temple's BlackBerry. 'Father Martin's number's there. I called that number right below it, the one marked CI?'

'Yeah?'

'It's a place called Classic Industries. Check out the address,' Tucker said.

Palmer moved to it on the BlackBerry and looked up quickly.

'Yeah, Woodbourne. Maybe we're starting to connect some dots here. I'll have Lily back at the precinct on it. In the meantime Wizner called to say Edith Zucker will be at this funeral parlor in an hour,' Tucker added handing Palmer the address. 'It's in Brooklyn. We might as well see if she knows anything that will shed some light on anything here.'

Palmer agreed and they headed out.

Because of traffic and some roadworks, it turned out to be a longer ride to Brooklyn than they had anticipated, but Edith Zucker was still there arranging the funeral for her sister when they arrived. She was accompanied by her son Carl and his wife Amy. They were all surprised that New York police detectives were interested in Ceil's apparent heart attack. They knew absolutely nothing about her confrontation with a so-called elder version of her son Bradley.

Edith was older than Ceil, but looked far less worse for wear. She was thinner, taller with dark brown hair in an elegant hairstyle. There wasn't a gray strand in sight. Although her son and daughter-in-law were there to assist her, she apparently was a firm, independent woman. Palmer thought that although there were clear resemblances in their features, it was still difficult to imagine Edith and Ceil were sisters, much less even related.

'I wanted to bring my sister's body back to Duluth. We have plots reserved there,' she began immediately after Palmer and Tucker introduced themselves, 'but she had left instructions to be buried beside Bradley and Preston. We really don't have any relatives in New York that will bother to come to a funeral.'

'Why are you interested in my aunt's death?' Carl asked. 'Everything points to congestive heart failure.'

'My son is a prominent attorney,' Edith said as if to justify him quickly asserting himself and getting right to the point.

'Is it true that none of you attended her son's funeral?' Palmer asked.

'We didn't know he had died,' Edith said. 'My sister told no one.'

'She was ashamed of him. We all were,' Carl said.

'Afterward, after she told you, did she say anything at all about his death, the events that in any way seemed unusual?' Tucker asked.

'What are you after here? The whole damn thing was unusual, if you want to talk about it,' Carl said. 'He was killed in prison where people are supposed to be guarded.'

'There is a possibility that someone is impersonating him,' Palmer said.

'How could anyone do that if he's dead?' Amy asked, inserting herself.

'Why impersonate him anyway?' Carl asked, grimacing. Then something clicked in his imagination. 'Unless, my cousin was involved with something very valuable and this person was trying to use his identity as a way to get his hands on it. Is that what's going on? Considering, few people knew or cared he was dead and buried, I suppose that's possible.'

'Maybe,' Palmer said.

'Well, how do you know someone is impersonating him? Who said so?'

'Your aunt,' Tucker said. 'That's how we got involved in this. She came to us.'

'Oh, poor Ceil. I tried to get her to move to Duluth,' Edith said. 'She was stubborn.'

'Look, here's my card,' Palmer said. 'Should anyone claiming to be Bradley Morris or anyone claiming to have seen him contact you . . .'

'Don't worry. We'll call instantly,' Carl said taking the card.

'No one has yet then or ever?' Tucker asked, to be sure.

'No way,' Carl said. 'Mom?'

Edith shook her head.

'Your nephew did have a pear-shaped birthmark on the right side of his neck, correct?' Palmer asked.

'Yes and very prominent too,' she replied. Her eyes widened. 'Someone who claims to be him has that?'

'Easily duplicated, tattooed ma'am,' Tucker said.

She nodded. 'How bizarre. Tomorrow, when we put poor Ceil in the ground beside her son, I won't be able to stop wondering if he is really down there.'

'Is there any chance he isn't?' Carl demanded sharply.

'A friend of mine in college used to say "in an infinite universe, anything's possible",' Palmer replied.

'That's no answer,' Carl countered.

Palmer shrugged. 'I don't have a definitive one yet, but when I do, we'll let you know. Thanks.'

They started out. Before they reached the car, Carl Zucker caught up with them. He actually reached out and pulled Palmer's arm to turn him. 'You two really disturbed my mother in there. What the fuck is this?'

'We honestly don't know the answers yet, Mr Zucker. We're just looking for clues. I'll tell you that the man either claiming to be your cousin or somehow is your cousin has killed four people since he confronted your aunt.'

Carl Zucker froze. 'How did he do it?'

'Three of them with a knife, apparently a kitchen knife.'

Carl nodded. 'Jesus.'

'What?'

'Didn't you go over the case, the reason he was sent up in the first place? He killed a garage attendant with a knife. It's always been his weapon of choice. My uncle put him under house arrest when he was ten because he slit someone's dog's throat. We used to joke about him and say he was going to end up being a world class surgeon or at least a butcher.'

They stared at him. He looked back at the funeral parlor and then at them. 'Maybe you should dig up that coffin,' he said.

'We don't have enough,' Tucker said.

'Not enough. Someone's using his name, has the birthmark on his neck and is killing people with a knife. What aren't you telling me?'

'There's a part of this we don't understand ourselves yet,' Palmer said. 'But I promise, as soon as we do, we'll contact you. Give me your card.'

Carl did so, but smirked. 'I got some friends here,' he said, clearly meaning it to be a threat.

'Lucky you,' Tucker said. 'I don't know anyone in Duluth.'

He and Palmer got into their car. Carl Zucker watched them drive off.

'Why the hell did we not pick that up with the knife?' Palmer asked. 'I didn't even read the transcript.'

'See?' Tucker said smiling. 'Good old-fashioned drudge police work has its place. Start being more like Charlie Chan and less like Kreskin.'

Palmer smiled. 'I just have to learn how to be both,' he said. 'We've got to locate this Gerald Spenser. Now . . .'

Tucker's phone rang. He listened after saying hello and then closed the lid. 'Well, lucky us.'

'What?'

'We're off the case. Foreman just said it's in the hands of the FBI. Something to do with those missing prints. But don't worry, he says, there's a new homicide case just dying for us to adopt.'

Palmer felt a great sense of disappointment. He looked back in the direction of the funeral parlor.

Actually, he felt more than disappointment. He felt betrayal and that weighed heavier on his conscience and heart.

'Mr Lords is regaining consciousness,' Mrs Littleton said calmly. 'I saw his eyes fluttering.'

Freda glanced at Shirley and then started down the corridor. Shirley remained at the desk, monitoring the other patients and reading her latest issue of *The Flash*, a rag magazine filled with half truth and innuendos about celebrities as well as candid photos. Some pictures looked doctored, however, and she wondered if they were doing digital enhancements and creations. If people could flock to fake professional wrestling, they would buy lies whether they were in print or in photos, she thought. After a while the line between what was true and what was false, what was real and what was illusion, would fade out altogether. Not enough people seemed to care anyway.

Mrs Littleton hung back. She was getting gun shy. Every time she opened her mouth lately, one or the other of the two nurses, and now even some of the supporting help, would either be critical or look at her as if she had violated all ten commandants in one swoop. She busied herself with some laundry and kept her mumbling under her breath.

Freda entered Louis Williams' room, of course believing him to be a man named Brad Lords. Why question the man's name or anything for that matter? His eyes were wide open and he was staring at the ceiling.

'How are you doing?' she asked him.

He didn't turn to her. He continued to focus on the ceiling as if he saw something up there. She couldn't help but look up herself. Although his arms and his torso were strapped in, he could move his forearms a little and open and close his hands.

In a move that took her completely by surprise, he seized her right hand, but in such a way as to clamp his fingers firmly around her thumb. It was apparently a grip he was accustomed to making, for he did it with a speed and expertise that took away her breath. In seconds, he had her thumb bent so awkwardly, she could feel the pain shooting up her arm and down her chest.

'Undo the straps or I'll break your thumb so bad you'll be deformed,' he threatened. 'NOW!' he cried and added enough pressure to get her to kneel.

She couldn't believe the pain.

'Don't yell or you'll be screaming, too,' he warned.

Quickly, she undid the strap that held his upper torso down and he sat up, now able to swing his right arm around and seize her hair. He pulled her toward the bed.

'Get that lower strap,' he ordered.

It was awkward, but she was able to undo it, too. He held on to her thumb and her hair and swung himself around. She was going to shout the moment he released her, but he was quite aware of that as well and in a fast, sharp, well-concentrated move, he drove his forehead into the bridge of her nose, snapping it instantly. The pain and shock overwhelmed her. Her eyes went back and she collapsed in his grip. For a moment he held her up simply with the grip on her hair.

Then he slowly lowered her to the floor and stood over her. They had put him in one of those stupid hospital gowns with the backs open. He went to the closet, but found it empty. 'This is fucked up,' he muttered.

He went to the door and peered out carefully.

Mrs Littleton carried a bundle of sheets down the corridor and went into the laundry room. Other than that, no one was in sight. He kept to one side and went down the corridor quickly on his bare feet. He looked into the laundry room and saw Mrs Littleton feed the sheets into a large washing machine. Glancing to his right, he saw a sack with a cord to tie it closed. He scooped it up and stepped up to Mrs Littleton almost in one uncut motion, wrapping the cord around her throat and tightening it before she could cry out. She gagged immediately and tried to stand. Pushing against him, she fell ungracefully on her rear end and he went to his knees to hold the cord deathly tight.

He couldn't believe the rush he was feeling. This was just like the old days. He had no aches, no pains. He was as strong as he could remember. The joy made him tighten his grip even more. He could see her eyes bulging, the saliva at the corners of her face turning red. Her body shook. She raised her hand in desperation and then died, so fast it was like puncturing a tire.

He lowered her to the floor and stood up. He didn't feel nearly as exhausted as he had expected. His hand burned a little, but that was nothing. Just out of practice, he thought. He went to the closet in the laundry and found a pair of white pants. They were a little short and tight around the waist, but at least he had a pair of pants and his ass didn't stick out. Mrs Littleton was wearing a blue sweater over her uniform. He stripped it off her and tried it on. He couldn't close it, but at least he had something.

Once again, he peered out the door carefully. The hallway was still deserted. What the hell was going on in this place? Why had they done this to him? What had they intended for him? He looked down at Mrs Littleton's body. He had no regrets. Whoever she was, she was in on it, whatever it was.

He started out slowly, keeping tight to the wall as he drew closer to the nurse's station. Shirley was still engrossed in her magazine. However, as he made the turn to go behind the counter, Freda Rosen, blood streaming down her face, stepped out of what had been his room and let out a scream so primeval, it even caused him to shudder.

Shirley spun around in her chair, saw him standing there, and cried out for help herself. Louis started to lunge for her, hesitated when he saw a pair of scissors on the counter, and went for them instead. Shirley cowered back, seizing a syringe to hold out in defense. He rushed her, easily gripping her right wrist and turning the syringe away while he drove the knife into her throat. She gagged on her blood and sunk slowly to her knees.

'Thank you, but I don't want a blow job now,' he said and shoved her to the side where she shuddered and slipped into her own dark tunnel of death.

He turned and stepped back into the hallway. Freda was still screaming. He considered going back for her a moment and then he turned and started down the hallway, the scissors gripped in his hands, one side of them out like a blade, Shirley Cole's A Positive blood dripping off them.

He reached the elevator and when he hit the button for the lobby, the doors closed. Feeling even greater elation than before, he had an overwhelming sense of immortality. He could kill forever and never be killed himself. He had felt this before in his life, but for some reason, never as strongly.

The elevator door opened on the first floor instead of the lobby. He didn't realize it for a moment and then he turned and saw the security guard standing there with his pistol drawn. He smiled at him. They won't kill me, he thought. They needed me for something.

He started to step forward when the gun went off.

He really didn't hear it reverberate in the elevator.

The bullet slipped silently through his forehead, shattering his brain and the back of his skull on the rear wall of the elevator. His body rained down around his feet a second later. The elevator door started to close, so the security guard put his foot in its way and it stopped.

Simon, terrified at the sound and the sight, came forward slowly, followed by Mrs Randolph. They all looked down at Louis Williams and the pool of blood expanding around his head.

'Damn it,' Simon said. 'What a waste of a specimen.'

Twelve

H e stood in front of the Waldorf trying to appear as casual and unexcited as he could. Every time a limousine pulled up in front, he stepped in its direction and watched carefully to see who the passenger was. He wanted to get to Henry Dover before he emerged from his vehicle, if that was possible. Finally, his continual presence in front of the hotel attracted the interest of one of the doormen, who strolled up to him and smiled.

'Anything I can do for you, sir?' he asked.

Bradley smiled back. 'I'm hoping to surprise my brother. I found out an hour or so ago that he was coming to the Waldorf for lunch today. We haven't seen each other for nearly a year. In fact, he doesn't even know I'm in New York. We both travel a lot and it's very rare that we cross paths.'

The doorman nodded. Bradley looked a little disheveled, but the clothes weren't cheap and the shoes looked new.

'In fact,' Bradley added taking out a fifty-dollar bill, 'maybe you would do me a favor and check to see if he arrived earlier than I was told. His name is Henry Dover. As I said, he has a reservation in the restaurant.'

The doorman's eyes widened at the sight of the bill. Fifty for just asking? 'Sure. No problem,' he said taking the money. 'I'll be right back.'

'Thanks. I didn't want to leave the spot in case he hadn't arrived, otherwise I would have checked myself.'

'I understand. I'm on it for you,' the doorman said and headed into the hotel.

Bradley smiled to himself. Money was clearly the key to the gates of opportunity. Show it, have it, spend it, or promise it and doors swung open. No matter what science does or how so-called powerful leaders alter things, that won't change, he thought. It didn't sadden him. It reinforced his core belief that the essence of all living things was purely selfish and that belief justified anything and everything he did in the past or would do in the present and future – if there was a future.

Another limousine pulled up. The driver nearly tripped over himself rushing to get out and open the door for his passenger. That urgency, near-hysteria to be prompt and subservient atti-tude alerted Bradley. He stepped off the curb just as the driver opened the door and he saw Henry Dover starting to rise from the seat to get out of the limousine. Bradley pushed the driver aside and pointed his pistol at Henry Dover.

'Thanks for picking me up,' Bradley said getting into the limousine. 'Tell him to drive on,' he ordered as he sat and waved the pistol at Henry.

'I have an appointment here,' Henry said nodding at the Waldorf. 'People will be looking for me.'

'That's been canceled. Tell him!' Bradley ordered.

'Michael,' Henry Dover called, eying the pistol. 'Please get back behind the wheel.'

Dover's chauffeur closed the door and started around the car. Standing on the curb, his eyes wide, was the doorman who had returned to tell Bradley Henry Dover had not yet arrived at the restaurant. The chauffeur looked at him with a clear expression of fear and then got into the car quickly.

'So, where are we going?' Dover asked Bradley.

Bradley didn't like Dover's calm demeanor even in the face of this threat. It further annoyed him. The arrogant bastard, he thought.

'Into the park,' Bradley said.

'Take us into Central Park, Michael,' Henry Dover told his driver.

The chauffeur started away, looking once more at the doorman who turned and headed back into the hotel quickly.

'So, Mr Morris, you've been on quite a rampage,' Dover said sitting back as if he was just going on a short, pleasant ride. 'Taking your anger out on poor Father Martin, as I under-stand.'

'And Jack Temple,' Bradley said. 'That's why I know you're appointment is canceled.'

Dover stopped smiling. 'You're crazy. You're making big mistakes.'

'As big as the one that was made on me? Tell me, did you

always know what would happen to me? Was I merely another sacrificial lamb wasted on your journey to riches and power?'

'We were, and are, addressing the problem. You were being given good care.'

'In God's Waiting Room. Thanks.'

'You obviously aren't the worse for it. You seem to be quite improved. That doesn't matter. We still owe you what you were promised and we'll deliver.'

'Oh, you'll deliver,' Bradley said. 'I'm going to want a lot more now.'

Dover smiled. 'Obviously. So negotiate. What do you want?'

Oddly enough, Bradley was the one taken aback. He had come to this moment too quickly and directly. He had been an enforcer, not a manager, and in a sense a blue collar worker who carried out the assignments he was given and then received his pay check. He had never created an assignment or been in charge of what was to happen next.

All sorts of romantic ideas flew through his mind to answer Henry Dover's question. Make Dover set up a Swiss bank account for him, buy him a yacht, or maybe just give him a million dollars right now. They all sounded good, but how could he guarantee and insure his own safety if and when Dover agreed to anything? He was familiar enough with pressure tactics and blackmail, but he needed something more. He was at least smart enough to realize that. And he could be as cool as Dover, he thought. An idea occurred to him. He knew where he could find his collateral for any promise.

'Take me to the clinic where I was treated and to this Dr Oakland. I remember his name,' he added smiling. 'In fact, my memory is just as good if not better than it was.'

'The clinic? For what purpose?' Henry said shaking his head.

'I'll be the one asking questions and giving orders, Dover. Just do as I say. The only thing keeping me from blowing your brains out is the noise and the possibility some of your blood will splatter on me.'

Dover finally revealed anger in his face. Before he could speak, however, his cellphone rang.

'May I?' he asked Bradley as he reached inside his jacket.

'It's not Jack Temple calling. I can assure you of that,' Bradley said smiling and nodded.

'Dover,' Henry said into his phone. He listened. His reaction was solely in his eyes and so subtle, it would take an ophthalmologist to discern it. 'When did this occur? I see. And the clean up? OK.'

He glanced at Bradley.

'I will be there. Consider my arrival a stage five,' he added and closed the cell. 'Michael,' he said leaning forward. 'Take me to the company.'

'Yes sir,' the driver said.

'The company? I said the clinic,' Bradley told him, nearly growling his words.

Dover remained calm. 'It's the same place, Bradley, and it is a bit of a ride, as you know. I did miss my lunch, too. I know this great Italian place on the way up,' he added smiling.

Bradley smiled too, leaned back and then in one swift, actually graceful motion, swung his arm and slammed the pistol squarely into Henry Dover's forehead. The blow opened a gash a half inch wide and was so quick and unexpected, Dover had no chance to block it. It stunned him and he slumped back to his right.

The driver hit the brakes, but Bradley lifted his pistol so it was in clear view.

'The back of your head,' he told him, 'is as big as a wall. Look at the windshield. That's where your eyes will be. Drive and drive fast but carefully,' he added.

The chauffeur pressed down on the accelerator, made a turn and headed for the West Side Highway.

Bradley sat back. Dover, regaining his composure, took out a handkerchief and held it to his forehead. 'You won't get away with this, Bradley.'

'I don't want to hear another peep out of you, Dover,' Bradley said. 'You just close your eyes and think about your estate planning in case there are any last minute changes you want to call in.'

Dover turned away. Bradley sat back. He was feeling strong again. Dover wasn't completely wrong about lunch either. At the moment that was the only regret he had.

They rode on crossing the GW, entering the Palisades Parkway heading for upstate New York. He was cutting through these powerful men as easily as cutting through cream cheese.

Damn, he thought, cream cheese on toast, some eggs and bacon. Why the hell did he think of that?

His stomach rumbled and that only made him less tolerant and angrier. It was their fault he was sitting here starving. He'd kill them all for that as much as for anything else. The driver, who periodically glanced at him in the rear-view mirror appeared to sense it. His hands clutched the steering wheel so tightly, the veins were embossed. It kept him from trembling.

He glanced also at Mr Dover. His handkerchief was soaked in his blood and he had his eyes closed. That shut the bastard up, Bradley thought.

The chauffeur looked, too. He liked his job and he loved the money, but he wasn't prepared to die for it. He was tempted to leap out of the car and run the first time they had to come to a stop. Of course, the lunatic might shoot him before he got out. That prospect, and not any remarkable loyalty, was all that kept him going. The smirk on Bradley Morris' face gave him the chills. It was as if the man could hear his thoughts and knew just how much of a coward he was.

Bradley nodded at him and he shifted his eyes away quickly. They passed the next hour silently. Finally, Bradley sat back and with his right hand brushed his hair away from his forehead. He felt something in his fingers when he stopped and looked down.

It was like a blow to his own face. Clumps of hair were in his palm.

What the fuck? I'm losing hair again?

He put it down between himself and the door quickly so neither of them would see and then he stretched his leg out and felt an ache travel in a ripple up his thigh to his lower back. He shifted uncomfortably in his seat. And then he had to clear his throat.

Slowly, Henry Dover turned his head toward him and lifted the handkerchief from his forehead and his eyes to look at him.

'What are you looking at?' Bradley snapped. His voice didn't sound as deep. The words seemed to rise from some small pocket of tightness in his throat.

Dover said nothing. He put the handkerchief back against his forehead and turned away.

Bradley flexed his arm and then sat quietly while a small

pool of terror simmered inside his chest and began to rise in temperature and bring his blood to a boil.

'Step on it,' he ordered the driver.

'We'll get a ticket. They're all over this highway with radar.'

'Like I give a shit,' Bradley said. 'Whoever pulls us over will be pulling over his last speeding car.'

The driver accelerated.

Dover kept his face turned away.

Bradley's heart thumped in slower, heavier beats. Why is this happening to me all of a sudden? I thought I was in some form of remission. More importantly, why in hell was this angry God giving up on him when he had been such a wonderful device of justice?

'Let it go,' Tucker said. He could see how deeply in thought Palmer was.

'Can you just let it all go?'

'What can we do, Palmer? It's in the hands of a higher authority. It's not the first time we lost a case to the FBI or the BCI. When I was younger, actually only a year or two younger than you, I was sure I lost one to the CIA, although no one would confirm it.'

'Why is this an FBI matter? It involves homicides in New York City.'

'You going into Foreman's office to demand an answer? I'm not. I need my head tonight. My mouth is in it and I have to chew my food carefully before swallowing.'

Palmer didn't respond until they were almost back to the precinct. 'This is not kosher,' he finally said and marched into the building.

Tucker said nothing.

Palmer continued toward his desk, his head down, until Lily Marshall stopped him. 'Got the information you wanted on that Classic Industries,' she said.

He looked up. He had forgotten he had asked her to do it. 'And?'

She handed him some printouts. 'It's a shell of some sort. It's holding a variety of LLC's under it, but I did notice that this man,' she said pointing to one of the documents, 'Henry Dover organized its articles of organization. I didn't check them all out, but he's down on the first three as the organizer as well.

'I knew you were going to ask about him next so I ran this off,' she said and gave him another document.

Tucker came up behind him and looked over his shoulder. 'What?' he asked.

'Classic Industries,' Palmer muttered. 'Information about the CEO, Henry Dover. Billionaire. International holdings, sits on the boards of a half dozen very influential companies. Hefty contributor to powerful politicians.'

'Big deal. Welcome to American democracy.'

'If you look at these companies on whose boards he sits, you'll see he has his hands in a lot of places.'

'So what? Put it away, Palmer. You're just getting yourself worked up for nothing. Our part in this is over. Be grateful. I'm sure we have enough waiting for us.'

Palmer shifted the papers and closed the folder. He didn't hand it back to Lily, however.

'Thanks,' he told her and walked on to his desk.

They picked up the report on the homicide assigned to them, the battering of a forty-four-year-old woman which looked like the result of a domestic dispute, and then went out to begin their investigation. Despite his effort to concentrate on it, Palmer found himself continually drifting back to the Bradley Morris case. Tucker was right, of course, he was just getting himself more and more worked up about it. It was that gut instinct thing, that intuitive sight that was telegraphing messages telling him something was very wrong about it, but what was he to do? He felt like a fireman chained to the fire station getting continual four or five alarms.

He stopped thinking about it when they got a lead as to where the husband of the victim might be and headed for a bar on New Scotland Road in the Bronx. It turned out to be an easy apprehension because the man had drunk himself into a stupor. His hands were still stained with his wife's blood and there were some stains on his shirt as well.

'I don't feel like I'm a detective as much as I feel like a garbage collector when we do one of these,' Tucker told Palmer after they stuffed the man into the back of a black and white and sent him off to be booked.

Palmer nodded but was strangely silent.

'Hey,' Tucker said. 'Why don't you take the rest of the day

off. I'll do the paperwork on this one. You can do the next human regurgitation that we're assigned.'

'OK, thanks,' Palmer said.

After they parted at the precinct, Palmer decided to drop in on Tracy at her office. It wasn't something he had done very often. In fact, he could count on the fingers of one hand how many times he had visited her there. Most of the time, she was too busy to entertain him anyway, but he liked watching her work. She was capable of doing two or three things almost simultaneously, holding the phone, working her Internet mail, talking to her secretary.

She had a beautiful office on the East side twenty-five floors up with her windows facing the East River. On the occasions when he appeared, he spent most of his time gazing out, watching the ant-like world below, the streams of traffic, the flow of commerce and industry that made this great city's heart pound with an energy unmatched anywhere else in the world. One time he smiled and hummed 'New York, New York'. Tracy had laughed and finally given him her attention then.

He entered her office and as usual found her on the phone. She held up her right forefinger, nodded at whatever was being said to her and then said, 'It's almost done. I'll give you the full report in the morning. No problem. No, thank you, Jeff. Bye,' she said and hung up.

'What, no crime today?' she asked him.

'Is Grant buried in Grant's tomb?'

'You know, I'm not going to swear to it. I've only taken their word for it,' she said, smiled, rose and went around her desk to kiss him. 'Hey,' she said pulling back. 'Something's not right.'

'What are you, a lip reader?'

'No, I'm a kiss reader. C'mon,' she said taking his hand and leading him over to her black leather settee. 'You want something to drink, a Perrier, coffee, juice, something hard?'

'No, I'm fine,' he said sitting back. After a moment he said, 'We were pulled off the case. FBI took over,' he added.

'What? Wow. Why?'

'I don't know.' He thought a moment. 'I told you about the missing fingerprints, right?'

'No. What missing fingerprints?'

He explained the failure to find them and then told her about Jack Temple.

'Jack Temple, the attorney? On the lower East side?'

'You know him?'

'I had a real estate deal that involved him. It involved some parking structures. He's a tough negotiator.'

'Was,' Palmer said.

'And you're sure it was the same man who killed him as well as the others?'

'Proudly announcing himself as Bradley Morris to Temple's secretary afterward,' Palmer told her.

'What was the connection to Jack Temple? I can't imagine any. He's so anal about his work, his only hobby is breathing.'

'I'm not sure how to connect the dots. I tied Temple to Father Martin and then . . .' He paused, reached into his inside pocket and took out his notepad, flipping it open with his thumb, 'To a high roller, power broker named Henry Dover.'

'Oh, I know who Henry Dover is,' Tracy said. 'He's into enough real estate to fill up any Third World country. He beat us out on a few deals over the past two years. I'm not so sure my boss, Mr Benson, doesn't have Dover's face pasted over his dartboard in his office,' she added. 'Very interesting. Do you think he's after Dover, too?'

'I don't know. As I said, we were pulled off the case.' He glanced at his notepad again. 'I was having one of the secretaries check on a company Dover runs, Classic Industries . . . turned out to be a shell for a dozen or so LLC's. It was interesting to me because it's located upstate, near Woodbourne where that penitentiary Bradley Morris was housed in is located.'

'Woodbourne. Wait a minute,' she said and went to her computer. 'Benson wanted to develop a housing complex near there for second homes. Yes, here it is. Dover was into that one, too. Funny, I never saw Classic Industries on the radar screen and I always research my opposition. Know thy enemy better than yourself. Seems like Chairman Mao said that or should have.'

'Apparently, Classic Industries doesn't do anything.'

'Henry Dover doesn't own anything that doesn't do anything, Palmer,' she said. She studied her computer screen. 'Did you get into any of these LLC's?'

'I told you. We were just pulled off the case.'

'I have great software for this,' she said, 'as you can imagine,' she added smiling at him. She continued to type and move her mouse about its mouse pad. 'Interesting. Henry is signed as the organizer of the articles of organization on all these LLC's.'

'Yeah, Lily told me that, but—'

'Except one. Henry never gives anyone anything for nothing, especially positions in his companies.'

'Which one?'

'It's just called Oakland, LLC. That makes sense.'

'Why?'

'Someone named Simon Oakland is down as the organizer of the LLC articles.'

'Is there anything else? What's its purpose?'

'Research,' she said. She looked up. 'Medical research. And its offices . . .' She went back to the keyboard. 'Its offices are at the same address as Classic Industries.'

'What can you find out about this Simon Oakland?' he asked leaning forward.

She went back to the keyboard. 'I've got a few, but there's one who is a Dr Oakland. He's published a lot. Two books . . . Jesus, Palmer.'

'What?' he asked practically jumping up at the reaction she was having.

'He's considered an expert in geriatrics with some very prominent and respected studies in Progeria.'

'Progeria? What the hell is that?'

'Premature aging,' she said. She returned to her computer and keyboard. 'In children.' She sat back. 'Perhaps a form of which Ceil Morris saw in her son?' She shrugged. 'A few more dots connected, but other than that . . .'

Palmer stood up. She thought he had a strange look on his face, an expression that actually frightened her. He looked like a victim of hypnotism, distant.

'Thanks,' he said and turned to leave.

'Where are you going?'

He paused at the door. 'We were taken off the case . . . as NYC detectives. Not as ordinary citizens. I'm going to visit Classic Industries.'

He started out.

'Palmer, you're not an ordinary citizen. Palmer!'

She rose and hurried after him, but he was already out of the main office and into the hallway for the elevators. She went out to catch him and saw the elevator doors closing. He managed to look out at her for a second before they closed.

She had the dreadful feeling she was seeing him for the last time.

Thirteen

Bradley felt himself slipping. It was truly like trying to stay in place while sliding down a hill of glass. He struggled against the urge to sleep and felt the sudden heavier weight of his eyelids. To hide his efforts, he turned away from Henry Dover and tried to keep out of the chauffeur's line of vision through the rear-view mirror.

Dover was still sulking over the blow to his forehead. Bradley had suspected he was more embarrassed about it than in pain. Here he was a kingmaker, a powerful businessman close to powerful politicians, ordering his servants about every which way he wanted and now, right in front of his driver, he is whipped into submission. Bradley thought the rage inside Dover must be close to exploding.

It would be in me, he thought.

Dover's cheeks did look puffy and he had squeezed himself into a tight ball against his side of the rear seat for nearly an hour and a half now. It gave Bradley pleasure to see it.

However, a frightening sensation similar to the numbness one felt when one's leg, arm or hand fell asleep was growing from Bradley's feet upward. It also resembled stepping into ice cold water. He couldn't help but shiver and each time he did, he checked to see if either of the other two had noticed. They were too deep into their own protective cocoons apparently. He was grateful for that, but now he seriously wondered if he would be able to move fast enough to keep them there when the time came.

His breathing became more troubled, too.

I feel the way I did just before I escaped, he thought. It heightened his terror.

'Which entrance should I take, Mr Dover?' the chauffeur asked.

'Rear,' Dover said with his face still turned away. His voice was muffled but audible enough.

Gradually, Dover began to turn around. They were drawing closer and closer to the property. Bradley fingered the pistol trigger. Or what he thought was the trigger. Was he on the trigger? Just that doubt made him sweat.

The limousine swung off the road to a gate and the driver hit a button above the rear-view mirror. The gate started to swing open slowly. Bradley sat up or thought he sat up. Did he sit up? Or did he imagine he sat up?

'Don't try anything stupid,' he said. Or did he think he had said it?

The limousine pulled up to the rear doors of the building. The two security guards, one of whom had shot Louis Williams, and the other who'd helped with the clean-up, stepped out, holding the door open.

'I'll kill you,' Bradley told Dover. 'Get them to drop their weapons and stand back.'

Dover was staring at him. Why did he ignore what he had just told him?

'Did you hear me, you bastard?'

Dover opened his door and got out.

'Not until I tell you,' Bradley shouted. He brought the pistol around.

'Tell them to bring the gurney,' Dover shouted at the security guards. The one who had shot Louis turned and went inside. The other approached the limousine and joined Henry Dover.

'What happened to you?' he asked.

Dover dabbed his forehead.

'You might need stitches,' the security guard said looking at the gash.

'What are you, a doctor now?' Dover said.

The chauffeur stepped out.

'Keep your eye on things, Michael,' Dover told him and headed for the rear door as the two attendants who had brought Louis Williams back rushed the gurney out of the building to the car.

Dover paused. 'Get him upstairs,' he said nodding at the limousine.

'Is he alive?' one of them asked.

'For now,' Dover said and walked in.

When they opened the rear door, Bradley almost fell out. One of the attendants caught him in time and scooped him under the arms. The pistol had fallen to the floor in the rear of the car. The second attendant saw it and picked it up, shoving it between his pants and hip. Then he helped load Bradley on to the gurney and they started for the building.

'It's amazing,' the chauffeur said. 'I mean, he wasn't a young man by any means when he got into the car, but . . .'

'Keep it to yourself,' the security guard told him. 'Don't let Dover hear you say a word.'

'I know, I know, but it's amazing,' he insisted as he watched Bradley roll away.

Maybe I'm dead, Bradley thought, realizing that none of the messages his brain was sending to his muscles were being received and acted upon. Maybe this is what death is . . . being locked in what you think is still your body, but you have no body anymore, just the eternally lingering memory of one. They put us in coffins, but we're already in a coffin, ourselves. We're trapped in ourselves!

He was shouting continually now, demanding, threatening and finally pleading, but no one noticed or paid any attention. Onward they rolled him. At the elevator, the attendants looked at him and at each other.

'I can't imagine how he walked out of here,' the one said to the other.

The doors opened and they wheeled him in, pressed the button for three and stood silently, both showing little interest in him now.

He cursed them.

We'll meet again, he told them, and we'll see how smug you bastards are then.

He was wheeled out quickly when the doors opened. Freda Rosen, wearing a neck brace, greeted them. Mrs Randolph quickly joined her.

'Room four,' Mrs Randolph ordered and they wheeled him into it and then transferred his body to the bed, dropping him unceremoniously like a load of firewood. He could feel great heat about him and wondered if he was approaching the gates of hell.

'This is exactly how he looked the last time I saw him,' Freda told Mrs Randolph.

'Um,' she replied, showing little or no interest. 'Get his clothes off and let's hook him up quickly. It doesn't look like Dr Oakland will get much information, but after what's happened here, we better be on the ball,' she said with a look that telegraphed the threat.

Freda nodded and quickly started to undress him. She pulled at his expensive suit and didn't care if she tore off buttons. She tossed his expensive shoes and removed his designer briefs.

'He stinks,' she said squinting. 'He smells like death.'

Mrs Randolph glanced back from the monitor cables.

'Tell me about it. We've had enough of that stench to fill Arlington,' she quipped.

Freda tried to laugh, but the pain in her neck stopped her instantly. She sucked in her breath and finished what she had to do.

Downstairs in their ER, Larry Hoffman treated and bandaged the gash in Henry Dover's forehead.

'You don't need stitches,' he said, attempting to make Henry feel better and less angry. His rage was less discriminatory now. He was snapping at everyone. He had called for Simon, but Simon had not yet appeared. He looked at Mrs Pearson.

'Where the hell is Dr Oakland?'

'He didn't pick up when I called his office, Mr Dover, but I left a message. Maybe he was in the shower or bathroom.'

Dover glared at the wall.

'Mrs Randolph called down a few minutes ago, Mr Dover. She said she didn't think the patient would last another hour.'

'Hurry this up,' Dover told Larry Hoffman. He finished the bandage.

Dover felt it and looked at himself in the mirror. The bandage covered most of his forehead.

'Damn son of a bitch,' he said to no one in general and stormed out.

The security guards had followed him into the ER and awaited orders.

'What the hell are you standing around here, for? Get back to your posts,' he told them and went to the elevator.

Upstairs in his office, Simon Oakland had literally fallen into a state of terror and depression. It truly looked like his whole world, his raison d'etre, had come apart. The events following Louis Williams' escape from his room were devastating on top of Bradley Morris' escape into society where he had already committed murderous acts. Mr Dover had made it clear that he had to plug up any other possible holes, and Simon had promised to get on it vigorously, a promise he had made in front of Senator Hastings.

Just this morning he had actually rationalized that something good had come from this reversal in Bradley Morris and then Louis Williams. It confirmed forever that aging was indeed to be considered a disease. That meant that the body's immune system had something to do with how quickly people aged, experienced and suffered the symptoms of age, and if that was true, as it apparently now was and could be proven beyond a doubt, then the possibility of stopping aging and even reversing it realistically loomed on the scientific horizon. He was a chief architect of this new vision, this new world.

I should still be congratulated, he concluded, and until this new incident directly involving Mr Dover, he believed in the end he would be.

Now what would he be?

The answer was obvious. He would be disgraced and discarded, sent with his bags packing back into a world where he would not only never again find any sponsors, but a world in which he would be held up to ridicule. All he had to compensate for his dwarf's physical stature was his medical, scientific standing, his respect in that community. All those who were afraid to even look at him askance and confined their jokes and remarks to some backroom would now feel emboldened. He would be mocked, satirized and never be respected, not only as a scientist, but also as a human being.

Henry Dover practically burst through the doorway. He stood for a moment staring at Simon who raised his head quickly from his arms folded on the desk. He didn't know about Mr Dover's injury and for a moment, he was mesmerized by the sight of the bandage on his forehead.

'Why didn't you come downstairs?' Dover demanded.

Instead of answering, Simon rose and started around the desk. 'What happened to you?' he asked.

'They told you I was in the ER.'

'But I thought . . . you were there with Bradley Morris. No one said . . .'

'So why didn't you come right down?'

'I was going to . . . I . . . haven't been feeling well and—'

'Don't bullshit me, Simon. Bradley Morris is upstairs on his last legs. You have what might be insurmountable problems now. The remission he experienced stopped and reversed itself in an almost magical way within an hour, it seemed. This process, or whatever the hell you call it, is a major fuck-up failure.'

'That can't be.'

'No, and I'm not standing here either. It's all in your fucking imagination.'

'Listen, listen,' Simon pleaded, 'I've been thinking about it and I might have an answer.'

'You might have an answer?' Henry Dover said calmly. 'You might have an answer. Bradley Morris killed Jack Temple. I just received a detailed report. It was a brutal murder. If anything, the man might have become a worse animal than he had been in the past. Maybe that's another unexpected result of your work. Look at the havoc and death Louis Williams caused here!' Henry Dover shouted, his arms out.

Simon knew it was his imagination at work, but he felt as if he was actually getting smaller in front of the raging, explosive Henry Dover. Soon, he would be impossible to see. He'd be less than an ant, less than those people he mocked out there in their beehive homes in the developments.

'I know. I'm . . .'

'Get your ass upstairs and do whatever you have to do to learn anything else from Bradley Morris before he dies. I have some calls to make. Go on!' he screamed.

Simon felt himself leap out of his skin and hurried past Dover. When he stepped out of his office, he saw Mrs Goodman standing off to the right looking at him. She reminded him of his mother after he had been caught spying on the girls in the girls' locker room at school and sent home. It wasn't a look of disappointment or reprimand.

It was a look of disgust.

Mrs Goodman retreated and he walked slowly, dejectedly, to the stairway like some general who was going to inspect the battlefield upon which his army had just been devastated.

Palmer thought about calling Tucker, but quickly rejected the idea. He had no illusions about his partner ignoring official procedure to follow up on a case they were ordered to drop, and possibly for good reasons. The FBI might have come across evidence to indicate that Bradley Morris' death records, prison records and criminal records were manipulated and there were criminal activities crossing state lines, perhaps even involving federal statues.

Palmer couldn't help referring back to the day he and Palmer had escorted Ceil Morris back to her apartment, to his intuitive sense that she was telling the truth, that she wasn't some poor, lost and confused lonely lady. Right from that moment, he believed she had indeed met her supposedly dead son and what had happened to him, what he was doing now, even if it went beyond the scope of anything he and Tucker had confronted, called to him, haunted him, would not let him just leave it be.

There were those who became so integrated with the system in which they worked that they had dampened any possibility of original thinking, and there were the admittedly rare and even rebellious ones like him. We don't get promoted as easily and as regularly, he thought. We cannot be trusted to accept and keep within the confines of the rules and regulations. We stir up the pot and so we are deliberately passed over, but that is a price we're willing to pay.

It doesn't make us prime prospects for a normal or so-called stable life. Maybe that was what Tracy had seen in him from the start and what made her, until just recently, hesitant about expressing any commitment, any hope for a relationship with longevity. What had caused her to change her mind now? Was her passion and love for him so strong that she would willingly risk happiness, or did she finally come to admire him for his courage and independence?

Was it courageous for him to be so stubborn and determined or was he simply and clearly not a team player?

How much easier it would have been to go home today as Tucker had? He was a good team player because he could turn it off. He could have a life outside of his work. He was not only willing to be that way, he appreciated that he could be that way. Tucker embraced all the limits, all the forbidden zones, all the unnecessary detours. They were his salvation. He was the straight-shooter's straight shooter. If anyone could be a nine to five cop employee, Tucker could be.

But I'm not Tucker, he thought. And God help me because I never want to be.

He sped up once he had crossed the GW Bridge. His plan was to see if he could meet this Dr Oakland and somehow get at what was going on here. He had no illusions about the man being cooperative, but he had faith in his own ability to get in between the lines, slip under the doors of no comment or subterfuge and scratch the surface of the truth. Of course, he had no concrete idea what that truth might be. All he knew was it had to be more than what they knew so far and that it involved people in high places and elaborate cover-ups. That was enough motivation to keep him moving forward.

When he reached the small hamlet, it struck him as odd that no one he went to in this very small community for directions had heard of Classic Industries. Did no one from the area work there? The clerk at the self-service gas station just shook his head. He claimed also to be a lifetime resident, but said he had heard only of Classic chicken farms. The two other customers lived in the hamlet, but one worked in Middletown, which was a city about thirty-five miles south, and the other was a second home owner. Neither had heard of it either.

He stopped in the village and went into a small grocery store, but the employees he spoke with there were recent, two of them possibly illegal aliens. They were both very nervous about answering any questions. The manager said he had a vague memory of the company, but he wasn't absolutely sure where it was located . . . on some back road out of the village proper was all he could offer.

Palmer was too late to speak with anyone at the post office. The doors were closed. The village was too small to have a local police station and he was unable to spot any law enforcement patrolling about the village proper this visit. He was getting very frustrated when he happened to see a postal employee pull out of the parking lot behind the post office. He started his car and went after him. The man was obviously annoyed and a bit frightened when Palmer leaned on his horn continuously until he pulled over.

Palmer drove up alongside and rolled down the passenger's window. 'Sorry to disturb you,' he said.

'What'dya want?'

'I need directions. No one I've spoken to seems to—'

'To where?' he asked, more annoyed now than frightened.

'I'm looking for a company called Classic Industries.'

For a moment Palmer thought the postal employee wasn't going to respond. He paused, gazed ahead and then finally turned back to him.

'We don't deliver any mail to that company,' he replied.

'What?'

'But . . . I know where it's located. It's off of fifty-two. They took over an old Catskill resort hotel and gave it a new face. Go straight about three miles and then look for a road on your left with a broken fence. It's about a half mile up that road on your right. Only reason I know about it is my brother works for the phone company and has been there.'

'That's great. I appreciate it. Sorry about frightening you.'

'I wasn't frightened,' he replied quickly. 'People around here use the horn more than the accelerator these days. Lots of second-home owners from the city,' he added and drove off.

Palmer laughed to himself, half amused and half refreshed by these simpler, no-nonsense responses from more rural people. He followed the man's directions and found the road, thinking how odd it was that it had no road sign. The road itself was pitted and cracked. At one point, bushes and some branches of trees extended too far and required him to pull completely to the right to avoid them. It was obviously not a road that trucks used.

And then suddenly it improved dramatically and there, looming ahead, was a four-story structure with a security gate. There was no security guard at the gate, but he spotted a call box. He didn't see any other cars in the parking lot in front of the building, but he did see a driveway that went around toward the rear. He also noted that the road he was on turned toward the rear, so he imagined there was another approach.

He understood what the postal employee meant about a new face. The building had a coffee white stucco and was on a small rise. Maybe in its heyday as a resort, it was a handsome structure, but now it was rather nondescript with only the small black letters spelling Classic Industries over the front entrance.

There was probably some real estate tax advantage to being

out here, Palmer thought and imagined a man like Henry
Dover would give high consideration to such things. He
reached over to press the button that would enable him to
reach someone inside the building. At least, he hoped there
was someone inside the building. There was no activity around
it and no sign of anyone present. He could hear the beep when
he pressed and waited. A dry, husky voice responded with a
not very friendly, 'What do you want?'

'I'm here to see Dr Oakland,' he replied. 'My name is
Palmer Dorian,' he added and then thought he might just be
turned away if he didn't say, 'Detective Palmer Dorian.'

'Just a minute,' he was told. Although the person he was
speaking to didn't sound at all friendly, he at least didn't
immediately say he'd never heard of Dr Oakland or Dr Oakland
wasn't there.

Palmer considered the building again. Behind the high fences
and with its electronic surveillance systems, it looked as formidable as a medieval castle must have looked to soldiers about to
storm it with their swords and bows and arrows. The late afternoon sun had fallen behind the structure. Shadows seemed to
rush at it from the surrounding forest and creep quickly up the
sides and front of the building, oozing around the corners and
toward the top. He was able to see the security cameras expertly
placed to cover a good portion of the area surrounding the property. A camera at the gate moved a little to capture him.

'Dr Oakland doesn't have you down for any appointment
today,' the voice said. 'What is this about?'

To come this far and be turned away would be too much
of a disappointment and too frustrating, Palmer thought. Like
some poker wizard, he decided to show his top card.

'It's about Bradley Morris,' he replied. It wasn't completely
a stab in the dark. There were all those dots Tracy helped him
connect, but how or why Bradley Morris would have anything
to do with Dr Simon Oakland and Classic Industries were
questions he couldn't answer yet.

This time the voice didn't reply. Instead, Palmer heard a
buzzing and the gate began to open.

Those were the magic words, he thought. There was no
denial, no 'we don't know what you're talking about', no one
saying he must have made a mistake.

He drove in slowly, parked in one of the spots designated

and got out of his car. For a moment he just stood there looking
up at the building. The windows were more like mirrors, dark
now, reflecting only the vague twilight.

As he approached the entrance, the door opened and a security guard stepped out. He could see a second one just inside
looking out as well.

'You have identification?' the security guard asked him.

He reached for his ID and flipped it open.

The guard looked at it. Then he raised his cellphone to his
lips and said, 'NYPD.'

He listened a moment and then stepped back enough for
Palmer to enter the building. The second guard didn't move.
He waited until Palmer was completely inside, and then he
turned toward the elevator. He pushed a button and turned back
to Palmer. The two guards were so close to him now that it
was as if they didn't want him to gaze too far left or too far
right. The elevator door opened and they all stepped in.

'Pretty tight security here, huh?' Palmer asked them.

Neither man responded.

The elevator doors opened and they led him out to the right,
stopping at a dark-wood double door. One of the guards
knocked and then opened the door and stepped back.

'Go on in,' he said.

Palmer nodded and entered Simon Oakland's office. The
two guards followed behind him and closed the door. From
the pictures Tracy had shown him on her computer, he recognized Henry Dover behind the desk.

'Detective Palmer Dorian,' he said. 'Please, have a seat.'
He indicated the chair in front of the desk. 'Dr Oakland will
be with us shortly. He's working on a little problem.'

'You're Henry Dover,' Palmer said moving to the seat.

Dover smiled. 'You know most people think fame, celebrity,
is something of value to pursue. They just don't understand
how disrupting and downright annoying it can be when you
are a serious, hard-working individual.'

'What happened to your head?' Palmer asked.

'Oh.' Dover touched his bandage. 'Stupid accident, I'm
afraid. Bumped into something I should have anticipated. That's
what happens when you don't keep your focus, Detective. I'm
sure you agree.'

'Absolutely.' Dover smiled and leaned forward.

'You're one of the detectives who was investigating the deaths of Father Martin and Jack Temple, were you not?'

'And a taxicab driver.'

'Oh, right, right. Well,' Dover said sitting back, 'wasn't this case shifted to the FBI?'

'How do you know so much about our work, Mr Dover?'

'Jack Temple was an associate of mine. His death was a major blow. It will be some time before I get over it.'

'Did you use your influence to have the case given to the FBI?' Palmer asked.

Dover just stared for a moment. 'Aren't you overstepping your boundaries, Detective? Why are you still pursuing an investigation when you have been reassigned?'

'I have questions I can't ignore. I'm one of those guys who keeps his focus, as you said one should,' Palmer replied.

If there was any lightness or any fragment of cordiality in Dover, it died instantly. His eyes hardened. 'So, this is something you're doing independently?' Dover asked.

'The FBI won't mind some free assistance. After all, don't we all want to solve these horrendous crimes? I'm sure you want your friend's killer brought to justice,' Palmer said. 'What do you do here exactly, Mr Dover? Inquiring minds would like to know.'

Dover smiled again. 'All in good time, Detective. Like good wine, good information needs to be finessed, aged with care, protected.'

The door opened and Simon Oakland entered. Palmer was not prepared to see such a small man. He wore his lab coat and carried a clipboard.

'Ah, there you are, Simon. This is Dr Oakland, Detective. Simon, this is Detective Palmer Dorian who is looking for information about Bradley Morris. He thinks you might know something about him. Am I correct, Detective? That was what brought you here?'

'Yes,' Palmer said. He started to rise so he could turn completely to Simon Oakland.

'Oh, don't get up, Detective,' Henry Dover said. 'Dr Simon will be happy to spend time with you. I'll get up instead,' Henry said rising to vacate the desk chair for Simon.

Palmer sensed his danger, but thought it better to pretend otherwise. He relaxed again.

'Dr Oakland,' Henry said indicating the desk chair when Simon didn't move.

Now Simon silently moved toward the desk, but Dover did not step away.

'I'm curious,' Henry Dover said, holding that cold smile, 'before I leave you two, how did you manage to connect Bradley Morris to Dr Oakland?'

'I didn't exactly, but I'm a fairly good poker player.'

'Bluffed on a hunch, then?'

'Well there were some dots that connected Father Martin to Jack Temple to you to Classic Industries and finally to Dr Simon Oakland.' He turned to Simon. 'I understand you're something of an expert when it comes to the study of aging, are you not, Dr Oakland?'

Simon looked quickly at Henry Dover, whose cold smile evaporated.

'Very good. You have, as they say, done your homework, Detective Dorian.'

'What is this all about?'

'It's about justice, right Dr Oakland?' Dover asked Simon who had come around his desk.

Simon paused, looked at Palmer and nodded. 'Yes,' he said, his voice barely above a whisper.

'We have good intentions here, Detective. We're trying to ease the burden on the penal system, the whole justice system, if you will. A few things have gone wrong, but we're trying to get back on track, right Dr Oakland?'

'Yes, that's right.'

'A few things have gone wrong? People have been murdered, a convict supposedly dead and buried might be out there raging. I would say more than a few things have gone wrong.'

'Yes, but it isn't for you to say now, is it, Detective? In fact, you have been the one to step over the line,' Henry Dover said. 'I'm afraid you have to go back to Go. Isn't that what we used to say when we played that kid's game? Only . . . I guess it's now a little too late to just go back.'

Now, certain he was in more danger than he had suspected, Palmer started to rise again, but this time, the two security guards were on him, holding him back.

'What the hell . . . ?'

Before he could do anything else, one of the attendants,

who had slipped in behind Simon, stepped up and stuck Palmer in the neck with a syringe. He struggled for a few moments and then felt himself sinking into unconsciousness.

'Well, here you are, Simon,' Henry Dover said nodding at Palmer, 'another . . . what do you call them . . . specimen?'

Fourteen

Simon watched the attendants roll Palmer Dorian out on the gurney and then turned to Henry Dover.

'He's a policeman. Won't someone come looking for him?'

'That's not your concern, Simon. What is your concern is the fact that he's here because of your miscalculations. Did you examine Bradley Morris?'

'He died about ten minutes go,' Simon said. 'But I was able to confirm my theory about all this,' he added quickly. 'It's a matter of dosages, finding the right formula. I believe I'm close now. I just need to have a little more time.'

'Well, you have two new specimens with him and Gerald Spenser. For now, we're going to have to rely on the old way of attaining guinea pigs, Simon, but there are too many people outside of our organization sniffing around, as you see. Without tangible results very soon, and I mean very, very soon, we're going to close it up.'

'Maybe we can move it all to another location, outside of the country, Mr Dover,' Simon suggested.

'I've thought of that, but it's a matter of the expenses, too, Simon. If this is all some work of science fiction . . .'

'It's not!' Simon replied, a little too forcefully. He knew that immediately from the way Henry Dover grimaced. 'Do you want something for the pain?' he followed, trying to show some concern and compassion.

'Yes, you're succeeding or getting the hell out of my life,' Dover said. 'Attend to your work.'

Simon nodded and turned around. He hadn't realized Mrs Pearson was standing there, too, and having her see him so berated brought a crimson heat into his face that was both embarrassment and anger. He marched past her and out the door. She looked at Dover and then followed.

He didn't want to say anything more to Henry Dover that

would in any way detract from his enthusiasm for the project, an enthusiasm that was hanging on by threads as it was, but the truth was that Gerald Spenser was a terrible specimen because he had tested positive for HIV. There were too many complications with his immune system to have any sort of value in working on him. For now, he just went through the motions with him and left him in a semi-comatose state. He expected he would terminate him. However, he didn't want to do it too soon after Bradley Morris' death. One after another like this was too damaging.

But this detective was another story. The moment he set eyes on the man, he felt himself chaffing at the bit. This man was a perfect specimen. Most of his specimens were sickly and dying from one thing or another in the beginning. How the hell did they expect him to make progress quickly with that, and then the inmates, although not suffering from serious ailments, were not the best possible specimens either.

He went up to the third floor. The attendants were busy removing Bradley Morris' body. He had no idea where they took these bodies. He didn't ask, not because he was afraid to ask, but because he didn't want to know. He wanted no part of anything but his work. He had to get back to that, to concentrate only on that and not bother thinking about what was going on out there. The truth was he was never very interested in what was going on out there. He rarely paid attention to any world or national news. He didn't read any magazines other than his scientific journals. He despised entertainment news. He was happy where he was and actually feared being moved out of there more than anything. He was just too comfortable.

Palmer Dorian was in room five. He approached it and watched Mrs Randolph and Freda Rosen preparing him.

'As usual, get all his vitals to me as quickly as possible. I want to run some blood tests,' he ordered. He could tell that Mrs Pearson, who was back at the desk, had told them both about his confrontation with Henry Dover. He saw it in the way they looked back at him, the lack of fear in their faces.

They know I'm vulnerable, he thought, that I need them more than I pretend.

This slippage in his hold and power over his personal assistants depressed him. He had to win back his authority and the only way to do that was to enjoy a remarkable turnaround. He vowed to do it.

'I'll begin preparing my treatments,' he told them.

Mrs Randolph actually smirked at his word 'treatments'.

Palmer moaned, but did not open his eyes.

'Isn't he regaining consciousness rather quickly?' Mrs Randolph asked.

'We can't sedate him too long and do what I have to do to start, Mrs Randolph. You know that. Just get him strapped in and everything will be fine.'

She nodded at the small table beside the bed. 'His things are there,' she said.

He looked at it. Palmer's identification was there, a money clip, car keys and his pistol with a small box of .38 shells.

'Why didn't they take all that?' he demanded.

'Mrs Pearson told them to remove the man in room four,' Freda said.

'There was no rush.'

'Apparently, there was,' Mrs Randolph said, obviously enjoying his displeasure.

'Well, get that all out of here now!' he ordered Freda. 'Take it up to the desk.'

She looked at Mrs Randolph.

'Mrs Randolph can handle this herself, I'm sure,' Simon snapped. 'Do it!'

'Yes sir,' Freda said, stretching the word 'sir' sarcastically.

He shook his head and retreated.

When he reached room three, he heard Gerald Spenser call out and realized he was fully conscious. Mrs Pearson came out from behind the central desk, a syringe in her hand.

'I have his first treatment with your formula ready, Dr Oakland.'

'Thank you,' he said taking it. This is a waste of my formula, he thought. I'm going to have to terminate this specimen. He entered the room and Mrs Pearson returned to the desk.

Gerald, eyes blazing with terror, turned to him. He was strapped in tightly.

'What's happening to me?' he asked. 'Why are you doing this?'

'We're only trying to help you, Mr Spenser.'

'What is that?' Gerald asked seeing the syringe in Simon's

hands. 'It's not the same stuff you used on Bradley Morris, is it?'

'Actually, it is, but it's not for you,' Simon told him, making a decision. He put the syringe down. He would save it for Palmer Dorian. 'However, you know you are HIV positive,' Simon said.

'So?'

'My work here has provided what is possibly a remarkable cure.'

'Really?' Gerald said calming, especially since Simon had put the syringe down.

'Yes. You know enough about my work through Father Martin, don't you? You know I've been experimenting with the human body's natural immune system.'

'Yes, I know. Father Martin thought it was all quite remarkable.'

'Did he? We had such little opportunity to talk, he and I, but I thought he was a very enlightened and perceptive man who was not appreciated.'

'Exactly. That's all true.'

'So, let me work on you a while longer and maybe we can do something nice for Father Martin. I'm sure he would have been very pleased to hear you were on your way to good health again.'

'Yes, he would. He was very fond of me and knew how much I respected him. It's just that the way I was brought in here . . .'

'I'm sorry about that,' Simon said. 'Unfortunately, I don't control that part of our enterprise. I'm just a mere scientist. I have to defer to the experts in politics, etc.'

Gerald nodded. 'Do you think you could undo these straps, Dr Oakland? I'd like to go to the bathroom and move about a little. Now that I know you're going to help me, I feel so much better about it all.'

Simon thought a moment. Where the hell could he go? He wasn't long for this world anyway, he concluded and smiled.

'Of course. Here, let me get you undone,' he said and unbuckled the straps. 'Just get back into bed when you're finished. I'm preparing your first treatment. I think we're both going to be very satisfied with the results.'

'Thank you, Doctor.'

'No problem,' Simon said. 'I'll send Mrs Pearson in shortly with something cold for you to drink. I'm sure you're hungry, too.'

'Yes, thank you,' Gerald said and swung his legs over the bed. 'I'm a little dizzy.'

'That will pass quickly,' Simon said. He took his arm and helped him stand. 'Get right back into bed when you're done,' he told him, picked up the syringe and walked out.

Gerald headed for the bathroom, but when Simon turned his back on him, he turned as well and headed out behind him just as Freda Rosen was passing with Palmer's things. The sight of him coming out behind Simon stunned Freda and she paused. Gerald didn't hesitate. He lunged past Simon and ripped the pistol from Freda Rosen's hands.

Her scream spun Simon around.

In room four, Mrs Randolph had just begun to strap Palmer's legs. She heard the scream and turned toward the door. When she looked out, she saw Gerald Spenser holding Freda Rosen against himself as a shield. The attendants had left with Bradley's body so there was no one else in the corridor but Simon. Mrs Pearson stepped out from behind the desk.

'What are you doing, Gerald?' Simon asked. 'I'm going to help you.'

Gerald smiled. 'Like you helped Mr Morris? I may be HIV positive, but that doesn't make me stupid, Dr Oakland. Get out of my way.' He waved the pistol at Mrs Pearson. 'You, too. Step back.'

All Simon could think about was Henry Dover's reaction to another of his blunders. How could this man have been so deceptive? He acted as if he believed every word.

I shouldn't have been so worried about telling Mr Dover Spenser was a bad specimen, worthless in fact, and should be terminated. Now look what I've done.

'You just give us that pistol, Gerald,' Simon said.

Mrs Randolph had stepped back and pushed the button to alert the security guards that they had a problem on the floor. That alarm was also flashed to Simon Oakland's office where Henry Dover was on the phone with his operatives. He was concerned now about Palmer Dorian's partner. It was promising that he hadn't come here with Dorian, but he wanted to be sure he was not pursuing the case any further, too.

He picked up his cellphone and buzzed security.

'What's going on?'

'We don't know yet, Mr Dover. We're heading up there.'

'Damn it!' Henry cried and rose from the desk chair. His head was pounding, but he had refused any medications until he was finished with what he had to do.

Meanwhile, upstairs, Palmer regained his senses enough to realize what was happening to him. He sat up and undid the strap around his legs as quickly and as quietly as he could. Mrs Randolph was just outside the doorway watching the scene unfold in the hallway. Palmer heard the commotion and slipped his legs over the bed. He saw his pants and shirt on the chair and went to them.

'Where do you think you're going, Gerald?' Simon asked. He thought if he just pointed out the logic and the facts here, Gerald Spenser would surrender the weapon and all would be good again. 'You're too far from any place to walk to it and you're not in any condition for all this anyway. What's the point of doing this? We're going to help you.'

Gerald put the barrel of the gun against Freda Rosen's temple and she screamed.

'Easy, easy,' Simon pleaded.

The elevator doors opened and the two security guards appeared, both with guns drawn.

'What the hell's going on here?' one demanded.

'Easy,' Simon told them.

Gerald walked backwards, taking Freda with him. 'Stay away or she's dead,' he cried. 'Stay back.'

As he retreated, Mrs Randolph stepped back in the doorway, but crouched like a panther to lunge at Gerald and pull the gun away from Freda Rosen's temple.

The security guards came forward. Simon stepped to the side. Gerald continued to back up.

Henry Dover appeared when the elevator doors opened again. 'What the hell . . . how the hell . . .?'

'Just drop the gun, sir,' one of the security guards said, 'and you'll be fine.'

Gerald shook his head and took a few more steps backward.

Mrs Randolph thought he was close enough. She lunged and seized his arm, pulling the gun from Freda Rosen's temple.

Gerald was so surprised by the action, he released the pistol
and it fell to the floor. Freda dropped to the floor as well and
the security guards fired at Gerald when Mrs Randolph released
his arm and stepped away. They hit him in the chest and
stomach and he bounced against the wall and fell.

The security guards lowered their pistols and looked at
Henry Dover.

'This is just too fucking much,' Dover told them. 'How the
hell did he get loose, Simon?'

Simon was about to start his defense when Palmer shot
forward, scooped up his pistol and rolled over to direct his
fire at the surprised security guards. He hit one in the shoulder,
spinning him around, and the other in the chest. No one else
moved a muscle and for a moment, no one spoke.

Palmer stood up straight, but still feeling some residual
effect of the sedative, steadied himself against the wall. Mrs
Randolph moved and he turned the pistol toward her. She
screamed and raised her hands.

'Get back in the room,' he told her, 'and close the door.
Now!' She did what he said. He looked down at Freda Rosen.
'Get in with her,' he told her and she hurried to her feet and
into the room.

He started forward. The security guard wounded in his
shoulder started to stand and raise his pistol again. Palmer
fired and hit him in the chest. He fell back against the wall,
stunned by his own death.

Neither Simon nor Henry Dover had moved a muscle.

Palmer waved his pistol to the right. 'You two and you,' he
said pointing the gun at Mrs Pearson, 'get into that room. Go
on.'

For a moment, Henry Dover considered one of the security guard's pistols, but then turned and walked into the room
once occupied by Gerald Spenser. Simon Oakland and Mrs
Pearson followed him in.

Palmer moved cautiously down the hallway to the desk.
There, he caught his breath and then picked up the telephone.

Inside the room, Henry Dover glared at Simon Oakland.
'Do you realize what you've done, all the work, all the people
you've put at risk?'

'You can stop it. You know the right people.'

'Yes, I can stop it at a certain level, perhaps, but you're

finished Simon. You should think about a job in the circus
working with midgets or other dwarfs. That's about the only
work you'll ever see after this.'

'Don't . . . tell me that . . . don't threaten me. I won't . . .
don't you dare talk to me that way.'

Henry Dover smiled at him and shook his head. 'I should
have realized at the start that you were a pathetic excuse for
a human being. Despite your so-called genius, you were just
too inferior to succeed.'

'I'll talk. I'll tell them about the people you've involved in
all this. You had better change your tone with me, Dover,' Simon
said. If he was going down, he would take them with him.

Ironically, Henry's rage was lit by Simon's referring to him
as Dover and not as Mr Dover. The frustration and the mess
this would all now cause blinded him to anything else. He
reached forward and seized Simon by the neck, shaking him.

'Don't you threaten me, you ugly, little—'

'Get your hands off me!' Simon shouted.

Like some cornered rat, he swung his arm around, driving
the syringe into Henry Dover's stomach and pressed the
plunger. It emptied quickly. Dover released his hold and
stepped back.

'Bastard,' he said looking at the blood spot widen on his
shirt.

'Calm down, both of you,' Mrs Pearson ordered.

'I'm sorry,' Simon said, 'but you were really choking me,
Henry.'

Dover glared back at him while Mrs Pearson attended to
the wound. 'What was in that?'

'Nothing,' Simon said holding up the empty syringe. 'I just
poked you. Sorry,' he said again and then like some trapped
rodent, he retreated to a corner. As did the other two, to wait.

Epilogue

Tracy was waiting for him outside the precinct. She sat on a bench in a small public playground watching children on the swings and merry-go-round. Their mothers sat off to the right and left chatting, most of them keeping a watchful eye on their sons and daughters. The chatter of the children reminded her of birds gossiping in some estuary. It was melodic and yet chaotic simultaneously. The only urban sound their voices didn't overpower were the occasional blaring horns coming from the taxicabs whose drivers were either impatient or showing off for their riders.

Some of the children assumed adult-like postures when they lectured or instructed their friends. Girls pressed a hand to their hips and tilted their heads. Boys pulled back their shoulders or put both hands on their hips and wagged their heads a little.

For a few moments in time, the world was miniaturized. How precious and how ironic these childhood moments were, Tracy thought. They were precious because they were gone so quickly and during them, you had no heavy thoughts, no pressing obligations and worries. They were ironic because you had no idea how valuable your childhood was and you continually looked forward to adulthood, impatient to be responsible for yourself and have all those privileges.

Suddenly, for the first time really, she was overcome with a great desire to be a mother, to be guiding and molding some beautiful child, dispensing all her wisdom and experience and partaking in the wonderful discoveries alongside her child, reliving the wonder of life itself.

It was almost as if she finally realized her full potential as a woman and that potential wasn't assessed in the way men measured their world, not at all. It brought a smile to her face and a yearning in her breasts she had felt only in dreams.

A wave of optimism washed over her, which was another irony because she was sitting here, waiting for Palmer to emerge from his cross-examination and possible severe reprimand from his superiors. He had, after all, disobeyed orders, despite the outcome, which was strangely absent from the news.

Palmer had described how the local police had been the first to arrive at Classic Industries, the officers shocked by the carnage. Federal officers appeared after that, descending, he said, like great buzzards to pick away at the dead. He was taken off in one of their vehicles for questioning. The two agents who asked him the questions almost seemed disinterested in his answers and descriptions. They were so indifferent, he thought, that he wondered if they were even real agents despite their identification.

He had to take control of his paranoia. It was stampeding at this point, he told her, so he just shut his mouth and waited for them to decide what to do next. He was practically flown back to New York in one of their cars. Someone else followed in his even though he assured them he could do his own driving and felt fine. No one listened. When they reached Manhattan, he was told to report to his commanding officer in the morning. They said his car would be at the precinct. Why they kept it overnight, he didn't know. He suspected it was being searched for something. But again, he put it out of mind to stop the paranoia. That's what he told her.

He had called her after he had settled in and gave her a brief summary. Even though he said he was going right to sleep, she arrived at his door twenty minutes after he hung up. He acted upset, but later, beside her in bed, he admitted he had been hoping she would come. He needed her near him. He had looked into the mouth of the great darkness and been able to pull back, but the impact of that experience would keep his skeleton trembling for a long time.

It was Saturday so she didn't have to be at the office, even though she wasn't above doing that from time to time. Palmer didn't want her to go with him to the precinct station. She had rarely been there. He called it the toilet bowl view of the city, ascribing that description to all the police stations.

'You don't need to be exposed to it,' he told her and for the most part, she listened and accepted it, but not today.

Today, whether he would admit it or not, he needed and wanted her support.

'I was right to do what I did,' he told her that morning. 'Who knows what I stopped, how many people I saved.'

She let him rant until he settled into a quietness that she recognized more as his strength than his weakness. He wasn't sulking now or steeping in fear. He was steeling himself, girding his loins, clapping on his armor. Let them come at him. He would be ready.

It was a beautiful enough day. She pointed to the bench. 'I'll wait for you there,' she told him. He nodded and she kissed him. 'I'm proud of you, you maniac,' she said which finally brought a smile to his lips.

'Tucker's not going to kiss me,' he said.

'Let's wait and see.'

He laughed and left her. He had no hesitation in his stride when he went into the station, but her heart was pounding in anticipation and worry for him.

She saw one of the little boys take a tumble off a swing. He didn't fall hard, but the surprise was enough to frighten him and start him crying. The other children watched him for a moment and when he saw they were, he sucked in his tears and nodded at whatever his mother told him, which was probably something like, 'You have to be more careful.'

For all of our lives, we hear our mothers telling us that, even in our dreams, Tracy thought.

Finally, Palmer stepped out of the station. She stood. It wasn't possible to tell anything from his damn stoic face, she thought. He crossed the street and came to her.

'So,' he said, 'apparently, whatever this is, it reaches into high enough places to make it difficult for anyone to really discipline me. They put on a good act, however. I had to look grateful and afraid. And promise I wouldn't do anything else concerning the matter. I was assured it was in the hands of the right people and the people responsible for doing bad things would be . . . what was the word . . . handled, I believe. Handled. What do you make of that?'

'An end to it,' she said firmly.

He laughed. 'You should have been in there with them.'

'I don't care. You've done more than anyone else. You have nothing to be ashamed about now by doing just what you're told.'

He had his hands on his hips and tilted his head just the way one of the little boys on the playground had and she laughed.

'What?'

'You never grow up, you guys. The games get more complicated maybe, but you're on this playground your whole lives.'

'And you'll always be telling me to be careful?'

She smiled. 'Yes, exactly.'

'Let's have a great lunch somewhere today,' he said. 'I'm paying.'

'OK by me.'

'And let's stop at this shop on the way. It's a nice day for a walk on Fifth.'

'What shop?'

'Something called Tiffany's,' he said.

She paused, a wide smile on her face. 'What?'

'Well you said the word engaged.'

She tightened her hold on his arm, laid her head against his shoulder for a moment and then looked back at the children in the playground.

Soon, she thought, soon.

Simon Oakland sat comfortably in the private jet and gazed out the window as they took off and headed for the Caymans. He didn't like how he had been unceremoniously rushed off as if he were some undesirable being deported. Someone, he wasn't exactly sure who, someone over Henry Dover, had given the orders. He was permitted to take his most valued personal possessions and everything necessary for his comfort and security was to be done. Dover didn't deliver that message. He wasn't positive about which agency the messenger belonged to, but he suspected the CIA or some clandestine division of it.

It didn't really matter what cards they carried or to whom they swore their immediate allegiance as long as they were doing what he wanted them to do.

'Another research facility is being set up for you,' he was

told. 'You made enough progress to keep everyone interested and willing to assist you in your work longer.'

He didn't know exactly whom to thank for that, so he just said, 'Please convey my appreciation and my gratitude.'

This whole mess wasn't really his fault, he thought, now that he was comfortable and safe and away from Henry Dover. It was Dover's failing. He should have had more security and been on top of things faster. I did my work and was doing it well. Someone more intelligent than Dover must have realized it.

He smiled to himself now. Dover was probably in the doghouse. Simon never really liked the man. He made the short hairs on the back of his neck bristle every time they confronted one another.

If I never see him again, it will be too soon, he thought.

He didn't ask after him. It was as if he never had existed.

Simon still prided himself on his cool ability to dispose of people whom he saw as unnecessary to his work, his goals. Sentimentality in the world of science was truly a weakness. He had lived this long without any affectionate relationships. He could live a little longer without them as well.

He looked back toward the rear of the plane. There was no one else with him but the two security guards assigned. One had his nose in some magazine and the other looked like he was already asleep. That was all right too. He never needed chatter to pass the time. He could do very well submerged in his own thoughts. He still had some important new calculations to make with his formula.

A little more than a half hour later, he heard one of the security guards get up and go to the restroom. When he emerged, he stood there looking at Simon. Simon's impression of the man was he was something of an oaf, one of their robots who followed through on his assignments mechanically, one of those hear no evil, see no evil types.

I suppose they have their purpose, their use, he thought.

He turned back to his notepad. He was so involved in his thoughts and work, he didn't hear the security guard come down the aisle. He realized after a moment that he was looking over his shoulder. He hated that. It was so damn annoying.

'Can I help you?' he asked him.

The man smiled. He had unusually big teeth, Simon thought and wondered what they could indicate about someone.

The plane seemed to bounce and then pretty clearly began a descent. Since it wasn't rapid, it was curious, especially since they were now over the ocean.

'Is everything all right?' Simon asked the security guard.

'I'll check,' he said and made his way forward to the cockpit. He opened the door and leaned in. Then he closed the door and made his way back.

'Cabin is now depressurized,' he said.

'What?'

The second security guard came up to join them. 'We've descended enough,' the first security guard told the second. He nodded.

'Hey, remember that scene in *Singing in the Rain* at the end when Debbie Reynolds is singing behind the curtain and they want the audience to know she is the real voice in the movie?' the second guard asked the first.

'Yeah, and they go arm and arm, singing the song and pull the rope that opens the curtain, right?'

'Yeah, that's the scene. I love that film. Whenever it rains, I start singing.'

The first guard laughed.

Then the second guard reached down and took Simon's arm.

'What are you doing?'

He started to sing, 'Singing in the Rain.'

The first guard reached over and grabbed his left arm. They both pulled Simon out of his seat. He didn't weigh all that much so it wasn't any great achievement. Then they lifted him literally off his feet.

Now both of them were singing, 'Singing in the Rain.' They carried him to the emergency exit.

The second guard reached over and pulled it open.

Simon's eyes nearly bulged out. 'Hey . . .' he began.

His scream rose back toward them from his free falling body like a parachute, only there was none and the sound died quickly.

They closed the door and the first guard returned to the cockpit to tell them they could ascend. He joined the second security guard in the rear and began to read his magazine where he had left off while his partner returned to his nap.

Somewhere below, seconds before he hit the water, Simon Oakland felt more disappointment than fear.

He wasn't going to be remembered after all.

Henry Dover ended his conversation with Senator Hastings and turned his chair around to look out of his office window. This is what the captain must have felt like on the *Titanic*, he thought. That was all right. He had done his best. It wasn't as if he would starve or in any way change his lifestyle. You win some; you lose some. If you want to be in the big games, you have to take big risks, he told himself.

There would be other opportunities and the ones who were deserting him now would regret it someday. One thing Henry believed about himself was he never forgot a favor and he never forgot a betrayal, no matter how small.

For now, he was safe and he had other things to do. No more doting on a failure.

He took a deep breath and then rose and stretched. He couldn't sit so long without moving around. It bothered his lower back. It always had a little, but today, more than ever. He scrubbed his face with his palms and ran his fingers through his hair.

The strands caught between his fingers surprised him. Sure, you always had one or two or even a few, but this was more like a clump of hair.

He hurried into the bathroom to look at himself.

The wrinkles in his face were deeper, as were the dark circles around his eyes and the web feet he had seen starting. More of his hair fell when he wiped it and he could see the graying moving up the strands.

A tooth began to ache in his mouth. Was it his imagination, or did his shoulders look smaller.

I'm shriveling up, he thought and then felt the small panic beginning in his chest. That syringe . . . that poke, as he called it . . . it wasn't empty, he realized.

He looked closer at himself in the mirror and for a moment as the evidence of advanced aging became even clearer and more prominent, he was positive he saw Simon Oakland smiling back at him.